The Widow's Locket

GHOST HUNTERS SOCIETY

Book Four

Adria Waters

For Dad.
My hero.

CHAPTER 1

MingkéHá sat atop his horse, his back tense and straight as he watched what remained of his tribe moving slowly toward the afternoon sun as it hung high in the sky. He stared at the fields of broken cornstalks and brown leaves of the other crops, burned by the relentless sun. He shook his head. Too many seasons of food dying on the vine. Too many seasons of the animals moving away. Too many seasons of his friends, his family, growing thinner and wasting away.

Turning, he glanced behind him at the mound where several members of the tribe were buried. He dropped his head, closing his eyes against the guilt. He was supposed to be their healer, the one who kept them safe. When the Headman fell ill, MingkéHá worked tirelessly to abate the old man's pain and make him well by using all the knowledge of healing herbs he had learned from those who came before him. Nothing worked though, and the Headman succumbed to the fire in his body, coughing up blood with his last breath.

Upon his death, the plan was made for the tribe to move to lands that were more fertile. MingkéHá, his friend, I^nthwé Théwe, and five of the Elders would stay behind to travel to St. Louis in a few days' time. The Elders decided after years of war, disease, starvation, and pressure from the United States government, to cede their land to the Ma'u^{n}ke, the white people.

He watched his people disappear over the horizon and then spun his pony in the opposite direction, his heels squeezing into the sides of his mount. The horse responded immediately and MingkéHá leaned down over its neck as it took off across the grassland. He would not give up this land. It was theirs and he would not be forced to leave. As his horse's hooves beat upon the dry earth, they strengthened his resolve. He would find the source of the blight on his tribe and stop it.

"MingkéHá!" I^nthwé Théwe called from behind.

MingkéHá did not stop, and he did not look back.

He rode for three days' time, the sun beating down on his back as he canvased the expanse of land that his people had called home for most of his life. He knew the land well: the scattered trees, the long, waving grass of the prairies, the gentle rise and fall of the earth's hills that appeared on the horizon like a giant spirit sleeping. MingkéHá traveled during the day and camped at night, the small fire creating a halo of warm light in the overwhelming darkness. While the fire burned, he practiced the healing rituals his Elders had taught him. Their voices whispered in his head as he touched and then rewrapped the contents of the small leather bundle he carried with him. His eyebrows drew together in concentration, his resolve renewed. He would find the bad spirit and keep it from harming his people.

His people.

MingkéHá felt a lump rise in his throat when he thought of his beautiful wife. He thought of her eyes, and about how they had burned with love when she looked upon his face, even at the very end. Her eyes had closed then, and her chest rose and fell with a final breath. Then, she was still. Forever still. Like so many others. That night, MingkéHá fell asleep with the cries of his dying people resounding in his ears.

The next morning, he awoke and cleaned up camp, burying the ashes from his small fire under the black earth. His stomach churning with grief and regret, he stood at the edge of the forest, staring down into a wide field below. From this vantage point, he could see the entire valley and the river twisting beyond, a ribbon of sparkling brown water winding its way through their land to the Osage's land to the south.

"Tandaré...?" He took a deep breath, the staleness of the air filling his lungs with a burning sensation. There was smoke on the air. His horse's nostrils flared and it tossed its head, stamping its feet on the ground.

"Xáp^a re," MingkéHá whispered, stroking its mane with a calming hand. He squinted against the rays of the rising sun, his gaze sweeping along the grassland below. A small plume of gray smoke rose into the air, almost dissipating upon the breeze. *Péje!* MingkéHá leapt onto his horse and kicked at its sides, spurring it into a gallop down the hill into the valley below. Flocks of sparrows took flight, their high-pitched warbles scolding MingkéHá as he rode.

As they approached the smoke, the pony drew up suddenly, rearing on its hind legs and nearly unseating MingkéHá. He nudged the horse forward, but it rolled its eyes and shook its head, balking again and again. Finally, he dismounted, landing silently in a crouch. He stood up and attempted to calm the terrified animal. Its nostrils flared and it backed away. The pony whinnied before running back to the shelter of the woods.

MingkéHá turned his attention to the smoke and waded through the tall grass, the tops whispering in the slight breeze. One step, then another. A moment later, he stood at the edge of a large circle of barren ground. A crease deepened on his face. Something was wrong here. The air was heavy with despair…hopelessness…death.

"Wanáxi," he said aloud, stepping into the circle.

The moment his feet met with the barren earth, a drowning sensation overtook him. MingkéHá gulped for air. He tried to jump back to the grass beyond the edge, but it was as if his legs were the great pine tree, bound to the earth through its deep roots. Gasping for a breath, he fell to his knees, the ground pulling at his spirit. He managed to look up, his lungs burning with the effort of breathing. His mouth stretched in a scream that rose into the sky.

Fighting against the onslaught of pain, MingkéHá inched forward toward the source of the smoke, intent on stopping this fire from catching and taking over the dry summer grass. In the center of the circle lay an object that glinted dully in the sun. He reached out, his fingertips touching the smoke that rose from the object. His breath was but a wheeze now and he could feel the life force slipping from him.

"MingkéHá!" A voice rose up above the prairie, carried by the breeze to his ears.

He tried to rise up to see above the ring of grass that towered above him.

"MingkéHá!" The voice came again, closer.

He recognized it this time. It was I^{n}thwé Théwe. A moan escaped his lips as he realized his friend had followed him, and had probably been following him for days. He had always watched out for the smaller MingkéHá since they were children. While I^{n}thwé Théwe had gone on to make a name for himself in battle, MingkéHá had stayed behind to learn the ways of healing with herbs and plants. Now, his friend was here, and he was in danger.

As the sound of I^{n}thwé Théwe wading through the grass got louder, MingkéHá pulled a breath into his body, preparing. The moment I^{n}thwé Théwe's head appeared above the grass, MingkéHá used his last breath to shout two words: "Sé^e!"

I^{n}thwé Théwe's face registered surprise and then horror as he obeyed the command to stop, his feet mere inches from the edge of the circle.

MingkéHá reached out and grabbed hold of the smoldering object. White hot pain seared his palm and he grimaced, gritting his teeth against the burning. Black tendrils of smoke wound their way along his wrist and then his arm, the muscles and tendons drawing taut as they seized. The blackness deepened as it rose toward MingkéHá's shoulders. With horror, he looked down and saw that his feet and legs were wrapped with long cords of undulating smoke. It crushed him, bearing down on his body with the pressure of a thousand choking hands.

As the toxic clouds reached up to caress MingkéHá's face, his heart exploded, sending a warm sensation throughout his body. He twitched, writhing on the ground in pain. His head lolled to the side and he saw his friend's frightened face silhouetted against the brilliant blue prairie sky.

It was the last thing he would ever see.

A rumble began from under the earth, shaking the grass with a sandpaper sound. The smoke rose up around MingkéHá, wrapping him in a cocoon of darkness. A moment passed, and then another and the rumbling overtook everything. Suddenly, the ground opened up and devoured his body. MingkéHá disappeared underneath the black earth of the prairie. The ground churned and boiled, sending up an angry dust cloud into the sky. Then, all was still and silent.

Iⁿthwé Théwe stood at the edge of the circle, recoiling in terror, as the grass along the perimeter turned black and floated away as ash in the wind. The barren area got bigger and he took a few steps back from the edge. A snake of smoke wound from the center, coming toward him with purpose. He froze, his muscles screaming with the effort that it took to keep standing there, facing the darkness that crept from the ground.

The wisp moved to his feet, obscuring the toes of his deerskin moccasins.

As soon as it touched him, a vision possessed him, overcoming his entire consciousness until he could no longer see the prairie. Only the vision. In it, MingkéHá stood straight and tall, his concentration on a wall of black smoke in front of him. He pressed his hands out against the darkness, driving it back. Iⁿthwé Théwe gasped as MingkéHá turned to look at him.

Go, my dear friend. I will hold it.

Iⁿthwé Théwe stood staring at his friend, his feet rooted to the spot.

"Gasún sdé ke." MingkéHá's voice was quiet, but strong.

Iⁿthwé Théwe shook himself from the vision. The smoke released its hold and plunged into the earth. The circle began to grow again, nearly doubling in size. Fear took hold, forcing Iⁿthwé Théwe back several feet before he turned and ran to the tree line. With a furtive glance at the blighted area in the prairie, he jumped on his own quick steed and drove his heels into its sides. It spun and took off, MingkéHá's riderless pony following close behind as Iⁿthwé Théwe rode toward his village and the elders.

He was miles away by the time the object emerged from the ground.

The tarnished locket lay forgotten in the sun, the painting of a woman's face behind the cracked glass in the frame staring out upon the land, waiting for its next victim.

CHAPTER 2

"Marissa! Wait up!"

Evie's voice followed me as I slipped through the snow, my feet pounding along in the footprints made by my dad's boots. Tears rolled down my face, freezing before they reached my chin. I wiped angrily at them with the sleeve of my coat. As I rounded a tree, I tripped and fell into a bank of snow. The icy fluff caught in my collar and wound its way under my scarf and along my neck as I scrambled back to my feet and started running again. My throat and chest burned with the frigid air.

Night closed in, pressing down on me with an almost physical weight. The tree branches caught most of the moonlight as it made its way through the woods to the snowy ground below, allowing only faint spots of light to illuminate my way. At the top of a small hill, I lost my dad's footprints and drew up short, indecision and fear paralyzing me. I stood rooted to the place, turning around in desperation, trying to find the lost trail. Andy, Tristan, and Evie almost caught up with me, but I spotted a footprint and I was fast on the trail again, ignoring the snap of the sharp branches as they reached out to snag at my clothes and face.

"Dad!" I screamed into the darkness as I ran. The sound echoed into the labyrinth of trees in the woods behind our house. *Why did I choose tonight to sneak out? If I'd been here...what? What would have happened if I had been here? Would I have been able to save my dad?*

Grandpa's words wrapped around me as I took a turn and slid down a hill on my rear end. *Marissa's in trouble. Come quick.*

What was he talking about? A vision slammed into my head and I stopped in my tracks, the group nearly running into me from behind.

I whirled around and faced them, their frightened faces gathered. "It was Sam!" I blurted out between painful breaths.

Evie reached out to me. "What was Sam, St. Louis?"

"He took my dad!"

A second before she touched my sleeve, I started running again, the muscles in my legs burning. I could see the glint of the moon playing on the icy creek below. *Almost there. He'll be there. He'll be there.* My nose ran like a sieve and I dragged my sleeve across my upper lip. *He'll be there.* I crested the hill and looked down at the creek below. It ran over the rocks and twigs, innocuously silent in the still night. My eyes followed the creek to the cave entrance.

Dad's footprints slid down the hill to the cave opening and then stopped.

"Dad!" I sprinted to the opening of the cave. The cave-in had completely covered the entrance, but I reached in, scraping at the frigid, unforgiving rocks. They didn't budge. I cried and clawed at the rocks for what seemed like a lifetime. The nail on my index finger gave way and pulled back, exposing the sensitive nailbed underneath. The cold air set upon it with frozen teeth and the pain blinded me. I didn't stop, though. I kept clawing at the rocks until I felt a hand on my shoulder.

I whipped around. "Help me!" I shouted in Andy's face. "Why aren't you helping me?"

I leaned around him to look at Tristan and Evie. They stood quietly behind Andy, their faces morose.

"I, we…" Evie began, but then her voice faded away into a sob. "I'm so sorry."

Tristan put his arm around her shoulders and pulled her into his side. He looked up at me. "We texted Grant."

"Good!" I spat. "Maybe he'll help me!"

I turned around and shrugged out from Andy's hand, beginning my assault on the unmoving rocks blocking my way from the cave. Another nail snapped off and I could see a streak of blood, dark upon the stone in the moonlight.

Andy knelt down beside me. His lips were a grim line as he began pushing against the rocks, trying to move them. Tristan and Evie came forward, crowding into the small space at the mouth of the cave. They began pushing as well.

Once, I thought I felt the tangle of rocks move a bit. A choked sound of hope wound its way up from my middle. Then, the feeling was gone and suddenly, I knew what my friends had known since they stepped out of the house to follow me through the woods.

My dad was gone.

I sat back, landing hard on the frozen ground. Wincing, I looked down at my mangled hands. They were stiff with cold.

"Here." Tristan sat down beside me and took his gloves off. He wrapped my injured hands in his own, spreading warmth through me.

"Thanks," I mumbled.

"St. Louis?" Evie's voice was small, uncertain. She cleared her throat. "St. Louis?"

I looked up at her. Her arms were wrapped around her chest, hands gripping her elbows. It reminded me of the time that she came to my house after her mother had kicked her out of the car. She looked scared.

Fragile.

The word popped into my head and stuck, knocking against my skull with persistence.

I took a deep breath, trying to quell the hopelessness gripping my soul. My chin quivered. "He's gone." My voice was a whisper, but the sound of those two words echoed in the little valley.

He's gone.

"We'll find him," Tristan offered. "It will all be okay."

I spun around, fury casting a red glow to my vision. "Really, Tristan? Is it all going to be okay? Are we going to go back to the house and find that he was just trying to teach me a lesson about sneaking out? We'll all sit around and drink cocoa and laugh about it?" My pitch rose with each question and I was practically screaming by the time I asked, "Who are you to tell me everything's going to be okay when you can't even figure out your own life? Enjoy Stanford next year!"

Andy took a step closer and opened his mouth, but Tristan let go of one of my hands and waved at him to stop. The cold air bit at my hand when he let go.

"She's scared," he said quietly. Then, he looked at me, his eyes intent upon my face. "Marissa, if Sam took your dad, then you know where he is."

My chin trembled again. "I know."

The image of my dad being pulled into the black mass clouded my mind. The pain he was in, the anguish of not knowing where I was, the feeling of failure...to me, to his parents, to my mom. It was all too much and I let out a noise that sounded like a wounded animal as I stood up, pulling my other hand from Tristan's.

"We have to find him," I said simply and started walking.

"Hey!" Evie caught up with me and grabbed my arm. I shook her off. "Stop it!"

"No, you stop it!" Her eyes blazed. "You stop running off and trying to fix everything by yourself! You stop thinking that you're all alone in this thing and treating us like the enemy! We," she gestured at Andy and Tristan as they walked up behind her, "are your friends and your family. And we will help you." Her eyes softened and her voice followed suit. "We will help you, St. Louis. You don't have to go through this alone."

Fragile.

The floodgates opened and tears burned my eyes before running down my cheeks. As my legs gave out, I fell to the ground. Evie rushed forward and sat down next to me in the snow, wrapping me in her arms as I cried. She rocked me back and forth and smoothed my hair back from my cheek like my mom used to do when I was upset. That small gesture felt so familiar and forgotten that it made me cry even harder. My chest hurt with the sobs that rose out of me, twisting around the naked tree branches into the winter sky.

Then, Tristan and Andy were there and their arms were around us. My friends held onto me, their huddle holding the pieces of me together.

When the tears finally stopped coming, I sniffed and then hiccupped and started shivering. We had been outdoors for hours now and the cold had taken a toehold in my body. My teeth chattered together.

"Come on," Andy said. He stood up with a grunt and then offered his hand to me.

I held out my uninjured left hand and he leveraged me from the ground. Tristan stood up, too, and helped Evie up from the snow.

"I'm sorry about what I said earlier. It wasn't fair." I looked up at Tristan.

He smiled. "I understand, but I want you to know that I *do* think it's all going to be okay. Things always have a way of working out."

You don't know that, but I wish I had your optimism.
I sniffed and nodded.

"We need to get you inside and warmed up," Andy said.

"I'll start a fire," Evie offered, "and Tristan can make some coffee."

"I need to check on my grandpa," I said.

Andy nodded and put his arm around my shoulders. I welcomed it this time and leaned against him as we walked, picking our way through the woods at the back of the farm. A blue glow lit the snow around me and I turned to see Evie looking down at her phone.

"Grant didn't answer," she said. "Do you want me to text him again?"

The roar of an engine reached my ears when I stepped around the corner of the barn. Headlights splashed on the barn and I put my arm up to shield my eyes. Grant's car slid to a stop in the driveway and he was out, running towards us. I felt my insides crumbling again when his arms wrapped around me. He pulled me close and I fell into him, the tears coming again.

"He's gone," I managed against his coat while Tristan, Andy, and Evie filled him in.

Grant held me at arm's length, dipping his head to look into my eyes. "Are you all right?"

I shook my head and blinked. As I did, movement from the house caught my eye. I turned to look at the open back door. The yellow square of light was obstructed by a shadow. A shadow that had a slight stoop, perfectly curled hair, and a wooden spoon in her hand.

CHAPTER 3

"Grandma!" I shouted, ripping from Grant's grasp and pounding up the back steps. I stopped, staring at her outline as she stood in the doorway. She looked faded, tired, and drained. I knew that look because I had felt that way myself so many times. I reached out to rest a hand on her arm. Electricity passed between us and my arm tingled with the exchange.

She lifted my hand from her arm gently. "I don't have much left tonight," she whispered.

I immediately felt guilty for siphoning off her energy and drew my hand from hers. "I'm sorry," I mumbled.

"Marissa?" Grant caught my eye. "Is your dad here, too?" His voice was quiet, hesitant.

I understood immediately. *If my dad's here and Grant couldn't see him, then that meant, well, that meant that my dad was...* I shook my head, not willing to allow myself to follow that line of thought any further. "No, he's not here, and neither is Grandpa." I turned and looked at my grandma. "Is he...?"

She pressed her lips together and took a deep breath, her nostrils flaring with the action. Her eyes darted to the table and I followed her gaze. A circle of smoldering spectral newspaper floated on the tabletop.

My eyes snapped back to her. "He's gone, isn't he? Sam took him?"

She nodded. It was a small motion that held more sadness than I could bear.

"I'm sorry," I said for the second time. The lump in my throat grew. *This is all my fault.*

"No, it's not."

I looked up.

Grandma's blue eyes burned with intensity. "It's not your fault. This started a long time before you, Marissa."

"But, if we hadn't have snuck out tonight, my dad..." My breath hitched painfully and I bit my lower lip.

"Your father and grandfather would have still been taken and you would have been as well, probably me, too. And, then, it gets what it wants."

I shook my head. "I don't understand."

She leaned forward. "You don't have to right now. I don't fully understand it myself yet, but that is for another time, and more importantly, another place. It won't be long before he comes looking for us."

"Sam?" My voice came out a squeak. The vision of him sprouting forth from the column of dark light within the portal took over my consciousness for a moment. His predatory eyes, ebony pools of empty hate that filled his entire sockets, coming for me. I swallowed and pushed the memory down. "What do we do?"

"We have to leave. We have to get out of town."

I shook my head. "I don't understand. I didn't think you could leave the house."

Her eyes took on a wistful sadness. "I *wouldn't* leave the house, not while your grandfather was here. He couldn't leave, but," her eyes darted to the empty kitchen table, "since he's gone, there is no reason for me to stay here."

Andy cleared his throat behind me.

"What's going on, St. Louis?"

"She, um, says that it's not safe here. Sam will figure out where we are and then, he'll come for us. We have to leave."

Tristan pulled out his phone. "I'll text my parents and yours," he jutted his chin in Andy's direction, "and tell them that we're staying at Marissa's tonight." His fingers flew over the keyboard. "Then I'll make a reservation at the hotel in Bethany."

"Better make it Chillicothe," Grandma said. "It's farther away," she said to me by way of explanation.

I passed the information on to Tristan and he nodded, still typing.

"What do you need to take with you?" Evie placed a hand on my arm.

I shook my head. "I-I don't know." *This is all happening too fast. What about my dad?* "My dad! I can't leave! What if he comes back?"

Grandma took a step forward, the scent of bacon and biscuits wafting up from her housedress. She held my hands in hers and took another deep breath. "He's with Sam now. He'll be fine for a bit," she added quickly as I opened my mouth to protest, "but you will be no help to him if Sam gets you, too. You understand that, don't you?" Her eyes never left mine as she waited for my response.

Pushing down the tumbling emotions that spun within my chest, I managed a small nod. *Dad's down there. In the darkness.*

"What did she say?" Grant's arm was around my shoulders then, comforting me.

"She, she said, um, that Sam has my dad. But we can't help him if Sam gets to me."

"Okay," Andy said, stepping into the middle of the kitchen, "this is what we're going to do. Evie, you go upstairs with Marissa and pack a couple of bags. Grab some warm clothes, phone chargers, boots, and anything else you think we might need. Got it?"

She nodded.

"Tristan will make sure the house is locked up and I'm going to get some equipment gathered from the basement. Grant is going to stay with your grandma here in the kitchen. If there's even a whiff of Sam, he'll yell."

"How will I know?" Grant asked.

"Oh, I'll let him know," Grandma said. Her jaw was set and her eyes were wary. "Go on, get your things."

Evie grabbed my hand and pulled me up the stairs. My feet weren't working very well and there was a dull thudding in my head. *What was Dad seeing? Had Sam twisted his memories yet? How were we going to get to him?* I stood in the doorway, watching Evie yank clothes from my closet. Then she shoved them in a bag she pulled from the shelf. *All my fault.* My stomach turned and I leaned against the doorjamb for support.

"...else?"

Evie's voice jolted me from my thoughts. I looked up at her. "Um, what?"

She stood in the middle of the floor, the bag at her feet. "I asked if you needed anything else." Her brow furrowed and she took a step toward me. Her voice dropped. "St. Louis, I know this is hard and I understand, I do, but you have *got* to be present. You have to stay with us here." She dipped her head to catch my gaze. "You get that, right?"

I nodded then cleared my throat. "I need to grab the book. It has all my drawings in it." I walked past her and grabbed it from the top shelf of my closet. "Maybe something in here can help us," I mumbled as I shoved it into the bag. "Go get your stuff and I'll get a couple of shirts from my dad's room for Andy and Tristan."

She gave me a worried glance and then headed through the bathroom to her room.

I stepped out into the hallway, the half-full bag hanging from my shoulder. I could hear the boys moving around downstairs, the floorboards creaking under their feet.

"Don't forget to turn the heat down," Andy called out.

"Got it!" Tristan responded.

I turned and headed along the upstairs hallway toward my dad's room. It took me a full minute to gather the strength to reach out and turn his doorknob and then another minute to turn on the light and step in. His bed was unmade, but only on the right side. My mom had always slept on the left. I walked over to his dresser, trying to shake the thought of my dad sleeping in a bed with my mom's memory.

Fragile.

I pulled open the top drawer. Socks. Shoving that one closed, I pulled open the one below it. I found an unopened package of white T-shirts and put those in the bag. As I reached up to turn out the lamp on the top of the dresser, the light glinted off a framed photo of my mom. She was sitting on a lawn chair at a family reunion and her head was thrown back mid-laugh. I reached out and picked up the frame.

The day came rushing back to me. It was a hot, sticky Missouri summer day and my grandma's side of the family had met at the City Park in Troy. We'd eaten a huge potluck dinner with potato salad, chips, barbeque ribs, Watergate salad, and about a dozen delicious desserts at the tables in the pavilion. After eating, the group spread out in circles of lawn chairs pulled from trunks and truck beds. Little cousins ran around, screaming and playing on the swings. Adults talked about the weather and the good times they had growing up.

I sat in a grassy spot near my parents, reading a book in the sunshine. I was too old to play with the little kids and too young to join in the conversation, so I read, snippets of their stories catching my ear occasionally. A welcome breeze rustled the pages of my book and I looked up to see my dad leaned over the armrest of his chair, whispering something in my mother's ear. Her eyes crinkled around the edges and she smiled and then threw her head back and laughed. The sound filled the park and made me smile.

I took a deep breath. I never realized how much I would miss that sound. I shook my head and placed the frame back on my dad's dresser reverently. As I did, I knocked something to the floor. It hit with a metallic sound and rolled across the worn wood, coming to rest against my boot. Leaning down, I picked up my mom's wedding ring and placed it back in its place on the ornate dish my dad had kept it in since she passed away.

"You okay, St. Louis?"

I turned to see Evie standing in the doorway, her arms full of clothes.

"Yeah. Um, yeah. I'm fine." Then I cocked my head. "Exactly how long are you planning to be gone?"

She shrugged. "Dunno. Want to be prepared for anything." She shoved her clothes into the bag and then pulled the reluctant zipper closed. She grunted and threw the strap over her shoulder. "You ready?"

I sighed and turned off the lamp. "I'm ready."

I followed Evie out the door and then stopped. I stood in the doorway for a moment, indecision freezing me to the spot. Then I stepped back into my dad's room and took my mom's ring, sliding it onto my finger as I followed Evie down the stairs to the kitchen.

"I'm going to throw this in the truck," she said as she disappeared out the back door.

I followed, my stomach turning and my nerves on edge. As my foot hit the linoleum, I recoiled. The air in the room was thick and oily.

Grant turned, his face white.

"What's wrong?" I asked, ignoring the feeling of dread and crossing the room to him.

He looked down and pulled the edge of his shirt up. The scratches from Sam were red and angry, oozing blood onto his shirt.

"It hurts more than it did before. I mean, it hurt, but not this bad," he said, lowering his shirt.

I looked over at my grandma. Her shoulders were tense.

"What's happening?" I asked.

She shook her head. "I don't know, but something has shifted. Do you feel it?" she whispered.

"We need to leave. Now. Andy! Tristan!" I shouted.

There were a couple beats of silence and in that time, I imagined the worst. My core shaking, I called out again.

"Front door's locked up." Andy walked into the kitchen. He burped and covered his mouth with his hand. "Sorry. The burger I ate earlier feels like it's trying to make a repeat appearance."

Tristan walked in behind Andy. His forehead shone with a layer of sweat. "Let's head out."

I grabbed the first aid kit from the counter where Dad left it after dressing Evie's scratches. I shook my head. That night seemed like so long ago now. *Her scratches had gotten worse before they got better, so maybe that was what was happening with Grant.* The thought didn't comfort me as I had hoped.

"Time to go, St. Louis," Evie said from the back porch.

My friends filed out the back door and I stood in the middle of the dark kitchen. The clock above the stove clicked in the silent house, measuring out the seconds. I stared through the dining room to the living room beyond. Dad and I spent that first weekend in the house eating peanut butter sandwiches together on the couch. His office doors were propped open and the light from the dusk to dawn light outside his window spilled in onto the floor. For a moment, I half expected him to walk out of the office, coffee cup in hand. He'd come into the kitchen and fill his cup, leaning against the counter while he said some goofy thing to me.

A smile turned the corners of my mouth and tears filled my eyes. *Dad.*

It took a moment for me to notice that the house was completely silent now. I glanced up at the clock and it was frozen, the small hand between the eight and nine and the long hand hovering near the six. Taking a step back, I pulled the back door closed and put the key in the lock. The mechanism clicked in the quiet night. The cold caressed the back of my neck as I stood looking through the panes of glass into the house, my hand on the key in the lock. *Like it's frozen in time.* The oily feeling spread from the door to the key and into my hand.

Movement from inside caught my eye and I squinted, trying to discern what part of the shadowy inside could have moved. I leaned closer to the windowpane, my breath casting a fog onto the glass as I peered through it. From inside, there was a sound like a gunshot and the window vibrated. I jumped back, my insides turning to ice as a handprint appeared in the fog my breath left. Icicles spread out from it, spider webs of crystals crackling across the glass. Yanking the key from the door, I turned and ran down the porch steps.

CHAPTER 4

Grant and I followed the red eyes of Andy's taillights down the twisting gravel roads toward the highway. We had decided to take the back roads out of town. Less chance of running into ghosts or Sam, I had pointed out. Grandma sat in the bed of the pickup truck, leaning up against the toolbox.

"How's she doing?" Grant asked. He drove with his left hand on the wheel, his right hand across his stomach.

"Fine. She doesn't feel the cold, so it's not a big deal."

He glanced over at me. "Still doesn't feel right to make an old lady ride in the back."

Grandma had insisted that we ride in separate vehicles. "That way, he'll only get one of us if we get stopped," she said.

"How are *you* doing?" I asked, shaking the thought away. Guilt washed over me as I looked at Grant's pale face. "Are you sure you don't want me to drive?"

He smiled. "I'm fine, really." The car hit a bump and he grunted, a grimace replacing the smile. He looked over at me. "Could use a few less potholes, though."

I closed my eyes and leaned back into the leather seat. My head hurt. The pressure built behind my eyes and my temples. I realized I was gritting my teeth and I opened my mouth, the muscles in my jaw tight and sore. "How long before we get there?" I asked.

Grant turned his wrist to look at his watch. "Usually, it'd take us about an hour, but I'd say closer to an hour and a half, two hours, going this way." He chuckled. "It'll go faster once we get on the highway."

I sighed and nodded. "We can stop along the way and get you bandaged up if you want."

Grant smiled again. "In case you hadn't noticed, we're not exactly running across a bunch of gas stations and quick marts out here." His tone grew serious. "I'll be fine. It's you I'm worried about."

I opened my mouth to say, "I'm fine," but shut my lips against the words. *Nothing was fine. Nothing. And all of it was because of me. Not only had we failed to help the ghosts and families that we were supposed to help, but now I had put my friends and family in danger. None of them was safe, and it was all because of me. All because whatever was under the courthouse wanted me.* I cleared my throat and stared out the windshield. *Well, if it wanted me, maybe I should give it what it wanted. I mean, what if I went down there? If it wanted me, then, maybe it would let everyone else go. If I went down there, maybe it could end this all.*

"What are you thinking about?"

I wrapped my arms around my chest. "Nothing." I swallowed. "It wants me," I said, my voice small.

Grant moved his hand from his stomach and placed it, palm up, between us. I took it, relishing the warmth and strength I felt as he wrapped his fingers around mine. He brought my hand to his lips and kissed it.

The gesture brought tears to my eyes. "I never meant to drag any of you into this."

"We know."

"If I went down there, maybe it would all be over. Maybe it would leave everyone else alone."

"You really think that would happen?"

I shook my head. "No."

"What *do* you think would happen if you went down there?"

"I don't know."

"If it wants you that badly, then you must be something pretty special. But, I knew that already." He shot me a grin.

"I'm not special. I just have this thing where I can see ghosts. What's so special about that? Why does it want that?"

"Maybe it's not the seeing ghosts part that it wants. Maybe it's the becoming a bridge for spirits to cross thing that it wants."

I stopped, letting Grant's words sink in. "Then, why is it taking everyone else?"

"Power. Influence. I mean, it's probably had you thinking about going down there, right?"

I glanced up guiltily. "Yeah."

"If it takes enough of the people you love, then you won't have any other choice. If you can bridge the gap between the worlds, it might use you like Evie did, to cross over."

I shuddered.

"And then where would we be?"

"We don't even know what *it* is," I said sullenly.

"Well, I'm pretty sure it's not a fuzzy unicorn with magical ice cream powers."

"Shut up."

He laughed. "I'm serious. Whatever's underneath the courthouse is not good. If you let it loose on the town…" He let the words hang between us. Then, he brought my hand up and kissed it again. "We're all here for you, Marissa. We love you and we're all in it for the long haul."

I sighed. "Remember the dream I had last night? I saw a lot of our, well, our ghosts when they were happy. Mary and Matthias were making plans to move to his hometown in Arkansas so they wouldn't have to live in fear anymore. Old Man Dietrich was talking to his wife after church, you know, before she was his wife. She and her family had moved to Culvers Grove and he was asking if he could take her out." I swallowed. "Then I saw my mom and dad meeting."

"Sounds nice," Grant said. He slowed his car as Andy flipped on his blinker up ahead. They turned onto another gravel road and Grant followed.

I hesitated. "It was, but there was something darker there. An undercurrent of danger." I glanced over at him and shook my head. "It's stupid. Whatever."

"What do you think it meant?"

I shook my head again. "I don't know. It was just a dream."

"How did you feel when you woke up?"

I remembered wrestling with the comforter on the floor. "I, um, fell out of bed and got tangled in my blanket."

"But, how did you feel?"

"Like it was trying to tell me something. Like I should have learned something from the dream."

"What'd you learn?"

"Why are you perseverating on this dream?"

He shrugged. "It's the second time you've mentioned it. It must have stuck with you."

"Oh." I looked up to check on Grandma. She was sitting in the truck, her face stoic and her eyes watchful. "Well, um, I guess I learned that love is pretty powerful and that you should hold onto the people you love while you have them."

"Where was your mom from?"

I side-eyed him. "Troy. Why?"

He held onto my hand while he reached down to shift as we hit a long straightaway on the gravel road. The land flattened out here and the country was visible for miles. Way up ahead, I could barely make out the lights of cars passing on the highway.

"We're almost there," I said.

"Stay with me for a minute," Grant said. "You said that something was keeping the ghosts here in Culvers Grove."

I nodded.

"Well, what if it only keeps some of them here?"

"Say more," I said, uneasiness settling in my chest.

"You guys tried to help Mary be with Matthias, but when you went back, he was gone and she was still stuck here."

"Yeah."

"Well, the same thing with Old Man Dietrich. If his wife wasn't from here, and he was, then that's why they couldn't be together. What if it's only able to keep people here that were born in Culvers Grove?"

His question lay heavily on the silence between us in the car. I ran through the idea in my head. *Mary and Old Man Dietrich were born here but their spouses weren't. Their spouses moved on, but they were forced to stay here.* "That doesn't make sense. Why were Amalie's parents still here? They emigrated from Germany. They weren't born in Culvers Grove."

"Are they still here?"

I shook my head. "They didn't move on until we reunited their family when we buried Amalie with them at the cemetery."

"What if they stayed because they were looking for something, too? When they found it, when you helped them, they got to move on?"

Matthias was here until I helped Mary let him go. Then he moved on.

Greta was here because she was waiting for Theodore. Then she moved on.

Amalie's parents were here because their children were in turmoil. When we helped, they moved on as well.

Grant's car picked up speed as we neared the highway. Trees rose up in the darkness on either side of the road and beyond that, fields lay quiet in the moon's silver light. I ran through everyone we had helped, and then shook my head. "What about Thomas? He was born here, but he isn't at the lake anymore. He moved on."

"What if he didn't move *on?* What if he," Grant paused and glanced at me, "relocated?"

"Sam was helping move spirits to other places in town?"

"You said Sam didn't want Thomas to be alone, that no one should be alone. What if he used the portal to get Thomas to his family?"

"I didn't see him at Melanie's house."

"Were you looking for him?"

"No."

"Then he could've been there?"

"But if people from Culvers Grove can't leave, then how is my grandma able to go with us?"

Grant shook his head. "I don't know."

I looked up to watch Andy's truck. Grandma sat up straight and turned to look toward the front of the truck. She started waving her arms frantically.

"Something's wrong," I said. I leaned up over the dashboard.

Grandma stood up, her eyes scared. Grant flashed his lights and Andy's truck slowed a moment before it shuddered and something knocked my grandma from the back of the truck.

CHAPTER 5

"Stop!" I shouted.

Grant locked up the wheels, his car skidding past my grandma's small frame as it rolled across the gravel. I was out the door as soon as the car stopped, my legs churning as I tripped my way along the icy gravel. At the edge of the road, I stopped, looking down at my grandma. She lay crumpled in the snow. She wasn't moving.

"Grandma!" I shouted. I tumbled down the ditch to her.

"I'm fine," she said before I got to her. She stood up and brushed her housecoat down around her legs. "Madder than a wet hen, though. What was that?"

"I don't know." I made my way over to her and grabbed her arm, helping her make her way up the embankment. Electricity sizzled between us, anger pouring out of her into me. She snatched her arm away when we reached the road and stalked off in the direction of the highway.

"St. Louis! What's going on?" Evie ran toward me. Andy's truck sat sideways in the road a few yards ahead of Grant's car.

"Everything was fine until we got up here and then something knocked her out of the truck."

"Is she all right?" Tristan panted.

"Yeah, she's fine. Just mad." I watched her walk away. "Come on. Grandma, what are you doing?"

Grant came up beside me while I walked. We followed her as she made her way toward Andy and the truck. About twenty feet before she got there, she put her hands up in front of her and slowed, taking tentative steps.

We caught up with her and I spun around to face her. The group moved toward the vehicles behind me.

"What are you doing? What happened?"

"Shhh," she said. She took another step toward me and I backed up. One more step and then she stopped.

She held her hands up, palms out toward me, feeling along an invisible wall. She looked like a mime pretending to be in a box. The image hit me funny, but I swallowed my giggle when I saw her face.

"What is it?" I asked, moving forward.

"I'll be darned," she whispered. "I didn't think it would work on me. Not that I ever tried to leave, but I always... I guess I always assumed I could."

"What's going on?" Tristan asked.

"It's like there's a wall here," I answered over my shoulder. "Like the one Thomas couldn't cross at the lake."

"But, your grandma has the same powers as you," Tristan said.

Evie was backing away up the road, her eyes on us as she went. I felt better that she was looking out for danger, watching over us.

"She's not as *alive* as you, though," Andy said. I turned to look at him. The color had returned to his face and he looked like he felt better.

"Andy," Tristan started.

"No, wait, he's right. Grant and I were talking about this. We think that the only people that can't leave are the people born here in Culvers Grove. She can move around a lot more than other spirits because she had the same powers as me, but she's still a ghost. She can't leave town."

"St. Louis?" There was a tremor in Evie's voice.

I whirled around, but didn't sense any danger. "What's wrong?" I asked, moving toward her.

"So, you know how I can see disruptions in the fabric?"

"Yeah," I said as I neared. "Do you see one here?"

She nodded, her eyes never leaving the direction we came from.

"A big one?" I turned to look. My grandma was still standing at the barrier, her jaw set and her hands moving along the wall, searching for a break.

Evie didn't say anything. Then she turned her eyes toward me. They were wide and she looked frightened. "That's an understatement. St. Louis, there's a bubble over the whole place."

"Do you see where it ends, where we can get my grandma out?"

She shook her head. "I don't think that's going to happen. It's over the whole town. Everything."

I shook my head. "Everything?"

"It surrounds the whole town and everything around it." She pointed to the left. "It wraps around as far as I can see that way," she pointed in the other direction, "and that way. It's around this whole place."

It keeps them here. All of them.

My blood ran cold and I shivered.

"And from the middle, toward town," she pointed off into the distance, "is the biggest spike I've ever seen. It goes so far up I can't see the end of it."

"Over the courthouse," I mumbled. My thoughts twisted in my head and I swallowed the lump in my throat. *My dad's there.* A thought flittered around the periphery of my mind, but I shook my head, trying to clear it. "I'm going to see if I can't get my grandma across." I took off, striding through the thin layer of snow that was already on the road. Big flakes had begun falling, the earlier clouds' promise fulfilled. I wrapped my coat around me as I came up to my grandma. I could hear Evie talking behind me, telling the group what she had seen.

"I think I know how we can do this," I said to my grandma, "but you're going to have to trust me."

She stopped feeling along the barrier and looked up at me. Her eyes flashed with annoyance. "I don't understand," she said again.

"Something bad is keeping spirits here. The ones who were born here. The ones from Culvers Grove. They don't have a choice to move on. They have to stay here. And," I sighed, "it's big, Grandma. It's the whole town."

She looked up. Then she wrapped her arms across her chest and turned to look back at the town. "I never thought it would come to this. I mean, there were stories about this place, stories of an evil spirit lying below, but I thought that's what they were…stories."

I crossed to stand next to her. "This isn't a story, Grandma. This is real and we're in danger. We have to get you out of here."

The wind picked up, blowing the snowflakes in eddies around me as they fell. The air between us vibrated and the same oily feeling came over me. The air thickened, making it hard to breathe.

"Something's coming," she said.

I felt my core begin to shake as the night fell silent. I could hear my friends talking, but their voices were muffled, as if they were coming through a layer of cotton. *Or the fabric between two worlds.* I felt bile rise in my throat as fear gripped me. Spinning around, I tried to locate the source of the feeling, an explanation for the sense of dread overtaking my soul. Grandma's eyes darted around, too, and she took a step closer to me.

"What is it?" I asked.

She shook her head. "I don't know. I've felt it before, though."

Realization plowed through my consciousness. I'd felt this way, too. When I got near the courthouse. Nausea wrapped its fingers around my stomach, squeezing, my head pounding with the sensation.

"Come on, we have to get you out of here," I said.

"What do you have in mind?"

I took a few steps back. When I could hear my friends' voices clearly, I knew I was on the other side. I put my hands up toward my grandmother.

She cocked her head to the side. Then, she shook it. "No, I can't let you."

"We have to try."

"I'll be fine. You all go on ahead to Chillicothe."

"No," I took a step forward. When I did, the sick feeling descended upon me again. This time, it was worse and I coughed, choking on the sick rising in my throat.

A sound reached my ears and I peered into the darkness along the road. Something was moving, but I couldn't make out what it was.

"Flashlights!" I shouted to the group behind me. "Over there!" I pointed wildly.

Andy plunged into his toolbox and brought out the biggest flashlight I'd ever seen. He flipped it on and turned it in the direction I pointed. I averted my eyes and squinted into the distance. The beam moved along the road, lighting it up in a bright circle. As he moved it to the far side of the road, it glinted off the snow and ice on a still pond nearly hidden by the trees. A figure moved out from behind a tree.

"Stop there!" I shouted.

Andy swung the beam back and it stopped, illuminating the small grove of trees nestled near the bank of the pond. I took a step forward, my eyes never leaving the spot. It took my eyes a minute to adjust and my brain a moment longer to register what I was seeing. I thought for a second that it might be the tree trunks moving, walking toward me. Then, as they broke from the grove, I realized what I was seeing.

They were people.

About seven of them from what I could tell. The figures trudged along the bank and came toward us, empty eyes never leaving my grandmother and me.

A strangled noise came up from my throat and I spun around. "Who are they?"

Andy flipped off the light so he wouldn't blind me. "Who are who?"

"Them?" I swung my arm in a wild motion toward the side of the road.

"St. Louis, we didn't see anyone but you."

Crap.

"Turn the light on again. There are seven ghosts out there, and they're coming toward us."

Andy's eyes widened and he thrust the light into Grant's hands before turning to grab his camera. Grant turned the light on and guided the beam toward the side of the road.

I followed the beam and my breath caught. They were gone. A noise reached my ears and I froze. "Over here!" I shouted, pointing about fifty feet away from me.

He swung the beam and I almost choked. The people had gotten closer; their eyes still intent and their gait jolting and twitchy. They walked like the zombies my friend Piper had shown me on a video about her favorite show. I clenched my teeth down on the whimper that rose from within.

"We have to do this, *now*," I said to my grandma.

She turned around, eyes wide with fear and nodded.

I took a step back, stopping when the nausea left. I placed my hands up toward the wall and nodded. Grant held the light on the side of the road, illuminating the figures as they drew closer. Grandma approached the wall and placed her hands up, meeting mine. With the barrier between us, the electricity I expected to feel was missing. I concentrated and reached through, locking my hands around my grandmother's wrists.

I pulled gently, guiding her hands and then wrists through the wall, the electricity once again passing between us. I felt strong, safe, and happy. "It's working!" I shouted. A feeling of euphoria passed through me.

Until I looked down.

As they passed through the barrier, Grandma's hands withered in mine, turning black and crumbling under my touch. Her mouth opened and she screamed, a dry, raspy sound that tore at my chest. I shook my head in horror and pushed her hands back into the wall. They returned to normal and she let go, cradling them to her chest, tears streaming down her wrinkled face.

I held my hands up and looked at them. "I-I'm sorry. I didn't know."

The figures were only about twenty feet away now, moving slowly but with intent. Panic welled up in me and I choked down a sob. "We have to get you out of there!"

"What's going on?"

"She can't leave! I thought if I held onto her hands, I could get her out, but it's not working!"

Tristan looked up at me. "Can she go into you, like Evie did?"

I spun around. "We have to try." I stepped into the barrier and grabbed hold of my grandma.

"What are you doing?"

"Come into me. I did it with Evie and she passed through me back into her body."

A sad slow smile spread on my grandmother's face. She shook her head and stepped away from me. "My dear Marissa, there's only room for one soul in a body."

A flash of the hospital room filled my consciousness. The memory of watching as Evie moved through my body and into her own. My shoulders fell.

Then, my friends were there beside me.

"We're right here, Marissa," Tristan said. He placed his hand on my arm. "We'll make sure you both get out."

I shook my head, the sob finally escaping. "The only way for me to let her in my body is for me to leave it."

"I'll be fine. Go to Chillicothe. Be safe." My grandma set her jaw and turned to face the approaching spirits.

"You can run. Get away."

She shook her head. "I've pushed too hard tonight. I barely have any energy left." She glanced over her shoulder. "Besides, it would only be delaying the inevitable."

I fell against Tristan, all the strength leaving my body. I was going to have to watch my grandma be taken. Just like Sarah. I couldn't bear it and I closed my eyes, allowing Tristan to lead me back toward the car. The sound of the spirits approaching was something that would haunt my nightmares forever.

Suddenly, I pushed away from him. "No! Get in the truck! Drive back toward town!" I launched myself into the bed of Andy's truck and hit the side of it. "Now!"

Andy blinked and then opened his door, throwing his camera on the seat next to him. He started the truck and pulled the door closed in one motion. The truck fishtailed, throwing me to the middle. I landed hard on my rear end and then scrambled back to the side. Andy drove past the rest of the group as they climbed into the car. Grant's headlights swung in a wide arc and then followed us, lighting up the bed of the truck and the area around.

I leaned around the cab, the wind bombarding me as I looked at my grandma. Tears streamed along the sides of my face as the icy wind burned my eyes. I blinked, never losing sight of my grandmother and the group of ghosts that were now almost in reaching distance.

"Hurry!" I shouted.

Andy hit the gas and sped down the road. Hooking my knees under the lip on the side of the truck, I reached out. *You'll only have one chance at this.* Pressing my lips together, I concentrated on my grandma's small form as she faced the ghosts. As we sped past, I leaned out and made a wild grab for her. I closed my eyes and gritted my teeth. My fingertips made contact with the back of her housecoat and I latched on, gathering the material in my hand and pulling as hard as I could.

I fell back into the bed of the pickup and my grandma landed on top of me, her small form bouncing as the truck hit a pothole. I held onto her, squeezing her against me, the electricity passing between us in a rush of happiness. I laughed and cried at the same time, holding her. I felt her arms wrap around me and she was hugging me, giggling like a child.

A moment later, we sat up. I looked out the back and saw the figures disappearing back into the grove of trees. Evie's face was almost pressed up against the windshield of Grant's car and I threw her two thumbs up, a wild smile on my face. Grant honked and flashed his lights and Andy slowed the truck a bit.

He slid the back window open. "You got her?"

"Yeah!" I laughed. "We got her."

The feeling of happiness lost its edge as suddenly as it had come, replaced by a pressing wave of nausea. I sat down and started shivering.

"Go on," Grandma nodded toward the cab of the truck. "You'll freeze back here."

"Where are we going to go?" I asked.

Grandma shook her head and stared back at the road. "I don't know where we'll be safe."

I shivered again, a motion that rocked my entire body.

"Go on. We'll figure this out."

I nodded and made my way to the back window. I took my heavy coat off, shoved it through the window first, and then snaked my way inside. My boot caught for a minute on the edge and Andy looked down at me while I was squirming upside down on his seat.

"Nice look, Anderson," he said. Then, he worked up a burp and shook his head. "I thought I was feeling better back there. For a minute anyway."

I yanked my boot from the window and buckled into the passenger seat. "It's the thing under the courthouse. It's how I feel every time I get near it."

"We're not going anywhere near the courthouse. Where should we go?" he asked, rubbing the back of his hand across his mouth.

"We have to get her somewhere safe."

"Know any good places? Near the border?"

"The border of what?"

He glanced over. "The border Patton was talking about. If we're staying here tonight, we need to be somewhere we can get you out quickly if things go sideways."

"My grandma, too."

He was quiet for a long time. "Anderson, you're my friend and I will try to keep your grandma safe, but if it comes down to choosing between you and her..." He let the sentence fade, but the implication was clear.

My phone buzzed in my pocket. I yanked it out, the crazy thought running through my head that it might be my dad checking up on me. The moment of hope faded quickly, replaced by a dull throb of pain. I swiped at the screen.

Evie. *Where are we going?*

I looked over at Andy. "Any ideas?"

He peered out the window. "Is it safe here?"

I scanned the countryside. The land was completely flat here and the road was situated between two large fields. "Yeah, I think so. I should be able to see anything before it can get close to us."

He tapped his brakes and then slowed the truck to a full stop. Grant's car stopped behind us and we all climbed out, meeting in a cluster by the back of Andy's truck.

"Where are we going?"

"It has to be somewhere safe. For Marissa and her grandma."

"Near the barrier or border. Evie, can you still see it?"

She nodded.

"I don't know where to go."

"We can't go back to the farm."

"We can't go to any of our houses. It'll expect that."

"I have an idea." My grandmother's voice was quiet but strong.

I turned to look at her. "Where?"

The group turned to look at the back of the truck. They were silent. Expectant.

"My grandparent's old place."

CHAPTER 6

We set off along the winding gravel roads, working our way northeast from town. I had insisted that Grandma join us in the cab so I could keep an eye on her and Grant followed behind with Evie and Tristan.

"Turn up here," Grandma directed. Her words slurred and I could feel the tiredness rolling off her.

I told Andy where to go and my stomach twisted painfully as Andy's truck rose and dipped over a small hill in the road. He burped and then coughed.

"It's up here. On the left. There's a driveway that goes over a small creek and then you'll see the house."

Grandma said. She finished talking and her head lolled back on the headrest.

"There," I pointed. The wipers brushed the large snowflakes off the windshield. It was really coming down hard now, a steady stream of fluffy flakes. The roads were covered in a few inches already and as we turned onto the unused road, I groaned.

"Yeah, his car will never make it." Andy put on his blinker and stopped the truck.

Frigid air filled the cab of the truck as he got out and walked back to Grant's car. I watched in the rearview mirror. Grant rolled down his window and talked to Andy for a minute. Then Andy got back in the truck, blowing onto his hands.

"He's going to park it back at the church parking lot." Andy put the truck in reverse and then turned it around on the road.

Grant turned his car around, too, and we followed them back to a quiet church we saw a mile or so back. Our tracks were the only ones on the road and they had already been almost filled in. We got to the church and Grant pulled his car into a parking spot near the front. They piled out and he locked the doors. Evie threw our bag into the bed of Andy's truck. I got out and waited for Tristan and then Evie to get in. They slid over, leaving a spot for Grant. I helped Grandma climb into the back.

"Be safe," I told her.

She nodded and rested her head on the toolbox. Exhaustion read across her features and my heart hurt for her.

Grant got in and I climbed onto his lap. He pulled the door closed and Andy started down the road, the going slow. He slid a couple of times, but the huge tires held. We got to the turnoff and he plowed through the drifted snow that came up nearly to the hood of his truck in places. His face was grim as he made his way along the path.

Grant's arms were strong around me and his breath warmed my neck. I settled into him. He grunted and I remembered the scratches on his stomach. I sat up, holding onto the dashboard so I wouldn't put any pressure on his middle.

"Thanks," he said.

The rest of the drive was silent. There was one heart-stopping minute when the front wheels of the truck crossed over the small bridge and the back of the truck began to slide to the side. I gripped the dashboard with white knuckles. Andy reached down and threw it into four-wheel drive and the wheels caught, guiding us across the rest of the bridge.

"She said the house was up here. Evie, do you see the barrier?"

She squinted out the window. "It's over there. About twenty feet. It winds up to the left behind that grove of trees."

I nodded. "It's close."

Andy powered up the last of the forgotten driveway to the grove of trees and then turned the truck around, facing out. "In case we need to get out of here quickly," he said as he set the parking brake.

"Everyone out," he said, opening the door. He hopped down into the snow and helped Tristan and Evie down.

Grant let me out and then stood by the car, holding his stomach.

"Are you okay?" I asked.

"I could use some ibuprofen," he said, "but I'm fine."

We made our way to the back of the truck, pulling out our bag and some supplies. I helped Grandma out and then looked around.

"Where's the house, Grandma?"

She pointed behind us. "Right up there."

I held onto her as we made our way through the snow to the house. The clouds had blocked out the moon and the walk was almost completely dark. Andy finally pulled out a flashlight and turned it on.

"Sorry," he mumbled. "Not really on the ball tonight, am I?"

Tristan wound his arm around Andy's middle, a look of concern reflected in the light of the flashlight.

We were almost on the front porch before we saw the house. A small one-story square building, it had a peaked roof and the clapboard on the siding had nearly rotted away. Nevertheless, it had a front door and the glass was still in the windows, at least on the front of the house. I hoped it was the same story along the back. It didn't look like it would be a warm night, but it was at least out of the elements.

Andy climbed the steps and threw his shoulder against the door. It shuddered and then opened. We crowded around him to get a look. The interior was rough, but the floorboards were intact and from what we could see, it was safe from the winter outside. I placed my grandmother on a ragged chair near the fireplace and she crumpled into it.

Andy headed in and shone the light around the front room. It was small and two doors led off the main room. They were both open and we found a tiny kitchen behind one and a bedroom behind the other. As soon as we stepped into the kitchen, the pressure lifted and I felt almost like myself again. The same happened in the bedroom.

"Evie? Do you see the barrier here?" I asked.

She squinted and then smiled. "It goes right through the house. Here," she pointed along a straight line that went a few feet into the living room and ran from one wall to the other.

Although we could still see our breath in the house, it was considerably warmer than the outside had been, and on the other side of the barrier, I began to feel more like myself. Andy perked up, too, and started looking at the fireplace. He began cleaning it out and Tristan found a broom and started sweeping the bedroom, making a clean spot in the middle of the room.

I took Grant to the kitchen and had him sit on the table while I lifted his shirt to look at the scratches. The angry red welts rose up, but the skin had closed along the scratches. I asked Evie to hold the flashlight while I used peroxide to clean the wounds. Grant winced a bit and I apologized, guilt pricking at me. He helped me spread antibacterial salve on the scratches and then we covered it in clean gauze. I gave him two ibuprofens from the bottle in the first aid kit and he swallowed them dry. Ripping open the package of T-shirts, I handed him one.

"Thanks, babe." He leaned down and kissed me.

The light in the room changed as Evie moved to the doorway. She clicked off the flashlight and her face was lit in a warm, orange glow.

"Nice!" she said and then disappeared into the living room.

Grant hopped down from the table, taking my hand as we walked to the doorway. Tristan had worked his magic in this room as well and it was void of branches and broken pieces of wood. He had placed a few chairs near the fireplace and Andy had a small fire started in the brick opening.

"I thought the flue would have been clogged, but it seems clear." He rubbed his hands together and held them out while he crouched near the hearth.

"Pretty cozy," I said. "Is everyone feeling better?" I glanced at my grandmother in the chair on the other side of the barrier. That side of the living room looked abandoned and cold. I shivered. "Will you be okay here?" I asked quietly.

She nodded and smiled. "I just need some time to gather some strength. I'll be fine in a little while."

"Yeah, as soon as I get outside the border, I feel fine," Evie commented. "I didn't realize I wasn't feeling well until I got outside and felt so much better. That's weird, right?"

"Not when you think about it," Tristan said as he sat down in a chair, putting his weight into it slowly to make sure it would hold. "If whatever's under the courthouse has been getting stronger, it would have taken place over a long time. We didn't feel like we were sick because our bodies acclimated to it so slowly. It's like someone with cancer. Most of the time, they don't even know they're sick until it's too late. By the time they feel bad enough to go to the doctor, the tumor's already taken hold." He glanced in my direction. "Sorry, Marissa."

"It's okay." I sat down on the floor and crossed my legs. Grant sat behind me and I leaned into him.

I took a deep breath. "I know why it wants me."

The group grew quiet, all of their faces turned toward me.

I cleared my throat. "What my grandma said tonight about only one soul inhabiting a body got me to thinking. I'm the only one that can create a bridge from one side to the other. I think it wants me so that it can get out of Culvers Grove. I think that by trapping souls here, it trapped itself and I'm its ticket to the outside world."

Everyone was quiet for a moment.

"That's creepy," Evie said.

"But it makes sense," Tristan said slowly. "You can move freely across the barrier."

"So can we," Andy said. "Why doesn't it take one of us?"

"Can *you* let a soul into your body at will?" Tristan countered.

"Oh. Not so much."

"I think you're on to something there, Marissa," he went on. "I think that whatever is down there has tried to take other people in your family because they can do what you can - or they could anyway. But since they're ghosts, they can't leave the town now either."

"What about her dad?" Andy asked quietly.

"He's forgotten how to use his powers," I said. Thinking of my dad made me sad. "He's not able to do that stuff anymore."

"And, you are."

"See?" Grant squeezed me from behind. "I told you that you were special."

I tried to smile, but my mouth wouldn't work.

"So, what's the plan?" Andy asked. He turned around and sat down near the edge of the fireplace.

I looked over at my grandmother. "I have to keep her safe. She's the only family I have left."

"We can't stay here forever," Tristan said.

I nodded. "I know."

"We have to figure out how to get to your dad," Evie said quietly. "Since the opening on the back of your property is caved in, we'll have to find another way in."

"Do you know any other entrances?" I asked my grandmother.

She shook her head. "I'm sorry."

I passed along the information to the group and then looked at my grandma and made up my mind. "Listen, guys, I think you should go to Chillicothe without me. If

I stay here, I can make sure she's safe and Sam doesn't get to her."

"How are you going to know where the barrier is?" Evie asked.

I shrugged. "I'll be fine. We'll stay on the outskirts of the town."

"I don't like that idea at all." Grant wrapped his arms around me.

"Can we talk about it in the morning?" I asked. "I'm exhausted."

"Yeah." Andy stood up and looked around. "Should we sleep in shifts?"

"Good idea. How will we know if something's coming, though? Only Marissa can see those things," Tristan said.

"I have an idea." Andy disappeared in the bedroom. I could hear him rustling through his bag. He came out with a box and recorder in hand. "We'll set up the spirit box and the recorder. That way, if Anderson's grandma gets in trouble, she can use the spirit box to talk to any of us."

"Brilliant," Tristan smiled.

Andy checked the batteries and then placed the box near my grandmother. "Can you get her to say something?" he asked.

I nodded. "Grandma?"

She waved a hand at me. "I'm not deaf. I can hear him just fine."

Her voice crackled over the box, snippets of words coming through in between the static.

Evie's eyes widened.

"Well, we've established that it works," Andy said. He sat back on his knees and looked around at the group. "Who's taking first shift?"

With Tristan sitting in a chair by the fire, we spread out the sleeping bags from Andy's truck. Evie and Andy bunkered down under their coats and Grant and I pulled his thick parka over us.

"You warm enough?" he whispered, his breath moving the fine hairs around my face.

I nodded and buried my head in his chest, allowing the sound of his heartbeat to comfort me.

He wrapped his arms around me, pulling me closer. "I love you, Marissa."

"I love you, too," I said against the fabric of his shirt. A few tears escaped as I took a deep breath and allowed my eyes to close.

CHAPTER 7

It felt like only a few minutes had passed before Andy was shaking me awake. "Your turn, Anderson."

I sat up, shivering as soon as the parka slid from me. "Already?" I stifled a yawn.

Andy wrapped his arms around his chest. "Yeah. You, then Patton." He moved over and burrowed under the pile of coats between Tristan and Evie. "I got more wood for the fire. You may want to throw one on in an hour."

I stood up and pulled a coat from the corner of the pallet. Grant grunted and turned over, his parka falling over his face. I smiled and stood listening to my friends breathing in the small room.

"They're good people."

I turned to look at my grandmother. She stood, her arms behind her back, her glasses reflecting the firelight.

I nodded and stepped over to the chair near the fire. The warmth radiated from the old bricks and I drew my legs up into the chair under me. "Yes, they are good people. They're my best friends."

Grandma continued looking at the pile of coats. "They care about you a great deal, don't they?"

I nodded again. A smile started, but then fell.

Grandma watched me. "What's wrong?"

I sighed and shook my head. "I've dragged them all into this. It's all my fault."

"Yes, it is."

My head snapped up and I looked over at her.

She chuckled. "Well, I don't much care for people feeling sorry for themselves."

"Is that why you didn't try to stop my dad from leaving after Thomas died?" The words were out of my mouth before I could stop them.

Grandma winced. She closed her eyes and took a deep breath. "I have more regrets than happy memories of the time your father lived here. I handled things the best way I knew how. I knew what he was going through, but I thought if I ignored it, if I helped him ignore it, it would…" She faded off.

"It would go away?"

She glanced up at me and nodded.

"It didn't. He saw his best friend die. Do you know how that feels?" My eyes snapped up at her. "Because I do. I watched Evie die. She was gone, but I didn't choose to ignore things. I chose to try to fix them because it's the right thing to do."

Andy snored and rolled over. I waited until his breathing was even again before I spoke. A million things ran through my head in those minutes, but I deemed them either too harsh or too soft.

"He needed your help," was what I finally settled on.

Grandma walked over to the chair and sat down, her face bathed in a shadow. When she spoke, her voice was quiet. "I was scared."

I blinked. "You were scared?"

"I was always scared. I saw ghosts when I was a little girl and my mother was too busy with her own problems to hear about mine. There was a man in the woods near our house. Later in life, I realized he was no longer living, but when I was a child, he was as real to me as you are. He lived in a shack near a creek." She smiled. "Mother would have been fit to be tied if she had seen that thing on her property. Everything in her life was perfect. Perfect house, perfect husband, perfect daughter." She paused, lost in thought for a moment. "I remember his name was Mo-Mo."

I raised my eyebrow.

Grandma smiled. "At times, I think I made him up, too, but he was my friend. He wasn't scared of what I could see, or do. It was the only place I could be free."

I watched as a tear ran down her wrinkled face, catching in a deep chasm near her chin.

"What happened to him?"

She looked up at me. "I don't know. I went out there one day and he was gone. The shack had burned down and all that was left were ashes." She took a deep breath. "After that, I decided that talking to ghosts or figments of my own imagination were a child's fancy, so I shut it out. I shut out everything. I went to school, got good grades, got a job, helped my parents, and took care of my mother."

"Was she sick?"

Grandma chuckled. The sound had a bite of iciness around the edges. "She wasn't able to handle the loss of my father's wealth with much, *grace*. In fact, I don't think she left her room for about three years, and during that time, I took care of her. My father worked as much as he could around town, but when he started selling the car and the furniture, she locked herself in the bedroom. When I would come to bring her food, she would be sitting there on the balcony, a book open on her chest, humming as she looked out over the fields."

"That's the way I saw her," I said quietly. "She seemed so nice."

"Oh, she was. She was so nice, so perfect that I could never live up to her expectations. I was always too outspoken, too genial, and too plebian for her tastes. On the day my father got a job at the newspaper in Chillicothe, he brought home a new car and honked at her from the driveway. It was like that fixed her. She had a purpose again. The Depression ended, my father made some good investments, and the house started filling up with expensive furniture again. I didn't fit in with the décor, so I left as soon as I met your grandfather. He was the son of a local farmer and completely and utterly reliable. His stableness was so far removed from my mother's flightiness that I got married to him the first chance I got."

"Did you love him?"

She smiled and looked down to pick at a piece of lint on her housecoat. "Not at first. I thought he was quiet and slow. But when I got to know him, I found out that what I thought was quiet was the sense to know what to say and when to say it. And what I thought was slow was actually the patience to think something through from all angles before acting upon it. He was a good man, and in time, I grew to love him more deeply than I could have imagined." Her eyes filled with tears.

I adjusted in the chair and brought my knees up to my chest, resting my chin on them. "I'm sorry he's gone."

She sniffed and brought the hem of her apron up to wipe at her eyes. "We all end up alone."

I stared at her. "What do you mean?"

"Our family. We all end up dying alone."

I sat up in the chair.

"I passed away on the day that your grandfather went to a sale in Davenport. I woke up not feeling well that morning, so he decided to drive up there by himself. He took the truck and trailer and I stood on the back porch and waved to him. I went downstairs to get a load of laundry out of the washer to hang on the line. I had the wet clothes in the basket and started to climb the stairs when I felt something seize up in my chest. Everything hurt, and well, I fell back and hit my head. I lay there for a while, and then I got up and took the laundry out to hang on the line. I heard the phone ringing all day in the house…it took me so much longer to hang the clothes that day…and then the ambulance came and I watched them take my body from the house. Your grandpa got home then and he was beside himself. I tried to comfort him, but he couldn't hear me anymore." Her breath hitched. "We were both alone."

Sam died all alone in the well.

"I'm so sorry."

How did Sarah die?

She wiped at her eyes again. "He came to be with me a couple weeks later. I was with him when he passed. I was waiting right there for him and we made breakfast. Just like any other day." She looked up at me. "I didn't want him to be scared. I never wanted anyone to feel like that."

"So that's why you didn't stop my dad from leaving."

She nodded. "I thought it was best if he left town, left all of those memories behind. He could start a new life and be happy. Away from all of this." She swept her hand out.

"Well, he did forget. He can't see them anymore. Even if he tries." My eyes snapped up. "How can you still do it if you ignored your ability?"

"Because I still used it once in a while."

I cocked my head to the side.

"Before your father was born, I had a baby. His name was Isaiah and he was beautiful. He passed away in his crib one night." Her words were clipped, filled with silent anguish. "We had him buried in the cemetery on the hill. I used to visit him and hold him. Sing to him. He was always so happy."

"Do you still see him?"

She looked down again. "Not for a very long time now. I didn't want to leave your grandpa."

I sighed. So much of her life was filled with sadness. Like mine. I looked up at her. "Thank you for telling me."

She nodded. "I felt like you needed to know."

"You said before that your mother told you stories about this place? This town?"

She nodded again. "One of the ones she told me most often was the one about the two brothers."

"Two brothers?" I yawned, my eyes pinpricked with tears. I blinked rapidly then leaned down to get a large piece of wood from the floor. I placed it on the edge of the fireplace, suddenly too tired to lift it any further. I sat back in the chair, my head dipping lower as the sound of my grandmother talking made my eyelids heavy.

"Long ago, there were two brothers. When they grew up and got married, they each built houses on the banks of a large lake near our town. The eldest son's wife coveted the younger brother and told her husband that he had cheated her out of her share of the family's wheat. When the eldest brother found out about this, he took the younger brother out to the middle of the lake on a fishing trip."

I yawned, my head dipping low on my knees. I checked my phone. Only about twenty minutes until

Evie would wake up to take over my shift. I blinked, my eyes burning.

"When they got out to the island, the younger brother began fishing and when he wasn't looking, the eldest brother got back in the boat and rowed away, leaving the little brother to die alone on the island."

"That's terrible," I mumbled, my eyes finally losing the fight to stay awake.

"It was. The younger brother was left on the island…alone..."

My head dipped again and I fell asleep, not hearing the rest of my grandma's story, or the door opening and closing a bit later.

CHAPTER 8

"Marissa!"

The voice jolted me from my sleep and I sat up, immediately on alert. The group was breathing quietly at my feet and there was no other noise in the house. I stood up and pulled my boots on.

"Marissa!"

My head shot up and I looked around, my breath coming in short bursts. I hadn't heard that voice in such a long time and everything about it felt like going home again. Tears sprang to my eyes as I crossed to the front door and opened it. It was almost dawn and the snow had finally stopped. The darkness was mediated by a pink tone. The promise of a sunny day to come was a whisper at this hour. Andy's truck was buried under almost a foot of snow and the noises of the woods were muted by the heavy blanket lying on its branches and crispy leaves. I stepped out onto the decrepit porch before pulling the door closed behind me. I stood there, my ears almost hurting with the effort of listening to the all-encompassing quiet.

Then, I heard it again. My name, called out from somewhere beyond the trees. I took a tentative step from the porch, from the safety of the group inside. For a moment, I thought about turning around and waking someone up, but then, the voice called again. This time, it was more insistent.

I shook my head. *I'll walk to the edge of the trees. If I don't see anything, I'll come back and wait for the guys to wake up.* With a decision made, I pulled my sweatshirt hood up and stepped down off the porch. Making my way to the edge of the woods was slow going. Vines and branches reached up, snagging in the laces of my boots and tripping me as I walked. I reached the edge of the trees and stood gazing out on a field. The driveway disappeared over a hill to my left, a line of trees hiding the end of it from me. I could barely make out Andy's tracks from last night as he gathered supplies from his truck and brought them into the house. The field spread out for miles, small groves of scraggly trees dotting it at intervals. A bird cried out, scaring me. I chuckled under my breath and chided myself for being so jumpy. The sick feeling had returned to my stomach, but this morning, after some rest, it was much more manageable. Nothing moved for several minutes. I gave up and turned to head back to the house when I heard it again.

"Marissa!"

I whipped around, searching for the direction from whence the voice had come. It was easier to locate out here in the open and I thought it came from a grove of trees in the distance. I looked behind me again. *Let them sleep. It's your fault that they're out here sleeping on the floor of an abandoned house instead of their own warm beds.* Guilt pricked at me as my feet moved, propelling me down the small hill to the open field.

Here, the going was nearly impossible. Without the tree branches to impede its journey, every single snowflake from last night's storm had found a place on the ground. The snow came up over my boots, spilling into them and within minutes, my socks were soaking wet. I shoved my hands into the front pocket of my sweatshirt and kept walking, burrowing my way through the snow. My heart was racing and I was breathing hard in no time. I stopped every once in a while to listen, but each time, I was greeted with only silence. The grove looked so much closer when I started, but each time I stopped to listen, it seemed farther and farther away.

When I was about halfway to the trees, a sound made its way to my ears. It was a song, a song that I knew from the depths of my heart. A song I had heard almost every night of my life until I was a teenager. A song I heard the final time last summer. I felt tears spring to my eyes again and I couldn't stop them this time. *You know it's not real. Don't get your hopes up, Marissa.* I closed my eyes, pushing down the hope that had sprung up like water from a busted dam within my core. Putting my head down, I pushed my way through the snow, determined to make it to the grove of trees.

A brook ran along the edge of the field, barely visible through the snow. The water had frozen and it stood still, mid-leap over large stones and eddies. The song got louder as I approached and I couldn't stem the tears. They ran unabated down my cheeks. My feet made craters in the blanket of white a foot deep. I stumbled along, trying to take the biggest steps I could without falling. The grove was only twenty feet away, ten, and then, I was there. I stood at the edge of the trees, peering into the large area inside.

"Mom?" I called out.

The sun rose then, bathing the grove in early morning light. I cocked my head to the side and then shook it. *I don't understand.*

In the area surrounded by tall trees was a village. The round houses were built of bark and dried cattails. Buffalo skins provided the doors and several people milled around, women and children talking and laughing near small fires. The weather was warm, almost muggy, and I pulled my hood off as I took another step forward into the shelter of the trees. When I did, I heard the thundering of hooves from behind me. I spun around and threw my hands up as several riders sped past on either side, the wind from their passage tossing my hair about my face. The thundering stopped and I turned to see women and children rushing forward to greet the men stepping down from their horses. There were many smiles and tears.

"Ragríwi ki," a woman said.

The man she stood next to dropped his head and shook it once.

I moved my foot, stepping on a small stick. It cracked like a gunshot in the quiet morning. The man turned to look at me. His eyes were dark, penetrating. Recognition crossed his face and he set his mouth and strode over. He stood in front of me, his eyes staring directly into mine.

"Hello?" I said, clearing my throat before saying more. "Can you see me?"

He narrowed his eyes and stared at me. When he did, the village disappeared behind him and took with it the warmth of summer.

I shivered and gritted my teeth against the chattering. "My name is Marissa."

He held his hand to his bare chest. "MingkéHá."

I looked around for a moment. "I-I'm sorry to bother you. I thought I heard my mom." My throat tightened and I blinked away another round of tears.

The man stared at me for another moment and then he took a deep breath. "Ugísa^n."

"I-I don't understand." I shook my head, wiping away my tears with the back of my hand. Cold wound its way to my core and I shivered again.

"Ú^{n}gisa^{n}re," he said again. This time, it was quieter.

I squinted. He was fading away, disappearing into the whiteness of the snow. "Wait! I don't understand!"

"Ugíssssa…" his voice faded away as a bright light spread out from his body.

I shielded my eyes with my arm and when I brought it down again, the man was gone. The early morning sun spread strands of golden light through the trees.

"St. Louis!"

I spun around, exhaustion taking over my body as my friends approached. Falling to my knees in the snow, I allowed the sob I had been holding back to escape. Tears flowed freely as Evie approached. When she reached the grove of trees, she wrapped my coat around me and Andy pulled me up from the ground.

"What's the deal, Anderson? We got up this morning and you were gone."

I ignored him and turned to Evie, grabbing her hands and holding them in my own. "What did the spirit board spell out?"

She brought her eyebrows together and shook her head. "When?"

I leaned in. "When you thought it was broken. It spelled one word over and over again."

"Oh, yeah. Um, G-I-S-A. We didn't know what it meant."

My breath hung in the icy air as I spoke. "I think we had it wrong. I heard Sam say that word when we were at the lake, but I think he was saying *Ugísaⁿ*." I stressed the oo sound at the beginning of the word. "Do you think that could have been what the board was spelling, too?"

Tristan flipped his phone around. It showed a picture of a board. "See how the U is right there? The planchette had to pass through it to get from A to G." He typed on his phone for a moment. "Doesn't say what it means, though, or what language it's in."

"I think it's a Native American word," I said.

The group turned to look at me.

"What's it mean?" Andy asked.

I shook my head. "I don't know."

"Marissa?"

I let go of Evie's hands and looked over at Grant. He stood next to a tree, resting his hand against the rough bark. His head was down, his hair hanging over his face. I took a step toward him, but stopped short when my eyes fell on his stomach. Grant had a hand pressed against the bandage I'd put on the night before. Blood spread from beneath his hand, working its way into a large circle of red on the white T-shirt.

"Grant!"

"I've got it," Andy said, stepping around me. He went to Grant's side and put his arm around his middle.

Grant looked up at him. "Thanks, man."

"Don't mention it." Andy turned to the group. "We need to get him out of here. Now."

Evie grabbed my arm and tugged. "Come on, St. Louis."

I nodded, bile rising in my throat, burning the sensitive lining. We had only taken a few steps across the field when I stopped. "I have to get my grandma."

"She's gone."

I turned to stare at Tristan. "What?"

"She left. Sometime early this morning." He began walking, but the unspoken accusation hung on the air. *She left while you were on watch, Marissa.*

I swallowed and followed my friends through the field. The way was a bit easier this time, as we were able to walk in our footprints, but I was still panting with the effort of wading through the uphill terrain in the deep snow. We made it back to the house in about half the time, and Andy and Tristan helped Grant into the truck. I stood next to it, indecision spreading through my stomach. It clenched and I broke away from Evie's grasp and ran toward the house.

Pounding up the steps, I threw back the door. It squeaked and then broke away from its hinges, falling to the floor, a cloud of dust rising up in its wake. I stepped inside, the mustiness of the living room clogging my lungs for a moment. The room was empty. I strode across the living room and peeked into the kitchen and the bedroom. Nothing.

"St. Louis? We have to go."

I spun around. "Where is she?"

She shook her head. "I don't know. I'm sorry, but we have to go. Grant's in pretty bad shape, and to tell you the truth, since we've been back inside the wall, I'm not feeling very well either." She stopped talking and a hacking cough spread through her, filling the space with the sound of sickness.

I nodded. "Come on. Let's get out of here." Guilt pressed down on me as I followed Evie out of the house and down the steps. *If Sam got to her...* I shook my head, not allowing the thought to continue. I climbed into the truck and scooted over to sit on Tristan's lap.

Grant was wedged between Andy and Tristan, his color gray. His head lolled to the side and rested on Tristan's shoulder as Andy fired up the engine and threw the truck into gear. Evie got in last and yanked the door closed behind her.

"Everyone in?" Andy asked, hiding a belch behind his hand. His eyes were watery and his color was off, too.

I nodded. "Yeah. Everyone's here." *Except my grandma.*

"Let's get out of here."

Andy's truck took some coaxing to get it out of its parking spot, but the snow bank finally released the tires and we slid down the hill toward the bridge. I pressed my arm into the dashboard, trying to stay as still as possible as the truck lurched down the hill. At one point, it twisted almost sideways before Andy spun the wheel, righting the truck moments before we hit the bridge. He crossed over and we made it to the road without further incident. I let out the breath I had been holding as he turned onto the main road and took off toward the church.

"Looks like they at least put some cinders down," he mumbled as he drove.

"What time is it?" Evie asked.

I glanced down at the digital readout on the dashboard. "Seven sixteen."

"It's Monday. We need to call out from school," she said.

Tristan handed her his phone. The truck cab was quiet as she dialed.

"Holy cow," Evie whispered as we pulled into the church parking lot.

"What's wrong, Patton?"

"Listen to this."

She put the phone on speaker and a woman's voice filled the cab: "Due to an outbreak of flu-like sickness affecting a significant portion of the student body, teachers, and staff, Culvers Grove R-IV will be closed until Monday of next week to prevent the further spread of illness. All school activities, including athletics, play practices, et cetera, will be canceled until that time."

CHAPTER 9

Evie helped me clear the snow off Grant's car while Andy retched into a snowbank on the side of the parking lot. Tristan had tried to help us, but ended up coughing until he nearly threw up before we ordered him back in the truck. As soon as the car was cleaned off and the windshield had mostly defrosted, I got behind the wheel.

Andy walked over. "Take it slow. Stay in my tracks." He cocked his head. "You got this, Anderson?"

I began a soundtrack in my head, full of hard-hitting music to pump me up. *You can do this.* I gripped the steering wheel and took a glimpse into the backseat where Grant lay groaning. *Correction, Marissa. You* have *to do this.* I put the car in gear and rolled slowly over the hill of snow we had created when we dug out the tires. It rocked gently as it came down on the other side and then, I followed Andy's truck out onto the road. I kept the tires squarely in his tracks and tried to keep my foot from shaking as it pressed down on the accelerator. When Andy came to the T in the road, he put his blinker on to turn left. I eased down on the brake pedal, the car responding and gliding to a stop. Up ahead, I saw Evie's head move and then Andy's. Tristan sat between, his head turning from one side to the other.

I glanced in the rearview. Grant was asleep, his face squeezed into a grimace of pain as he breathed unevenly. The blood continued to spread and I was worried he would bleed out before we could get him out of town. I looked ahead and hit the horn. Evie turned to look at me and then she gestured to the right. Andy switched his blinker and turned right, his tires spinning on the slick road. I stepped down on the pedal and had a moment of panic as the rear wheels spun, pointing the nose of the car toward the ditch. I pulled my foot from the pedal and took a deep breath. I pushed down again, slower this time, and the wheels caught and the car turned the corner, following Andy up the road. We drove for about three miles and the country spread out a bit, fields of snow flanking us. When I saw the highway up ahead, I suddenly knew what the disagreement had been at the stop sign. Andy had wanted to stick to the back roads, but Evie wanted to cut down on time by hitting the highway.

Good choice, Evie, I thought, as we crossed over the viaduct and turned onto the ramp. I breathed out a huge sigh as I caught sight of the gray pavement shining in the sun. The snowplows had been through here and the right lane was nearly clear. We drove several miles up the highway, the tires humming on the pavement.

"Hey." Grant's voice was grainy and muffled.

I looked in the mirror. He was sitting up and there was color in his cheeks. "Are you okay?" I asked.

"Yeah. Not a hundred percent, but better." He grunted as he reached to pull up his shirt.

I swallowed and turned my eyes back to the road. "Has it stopped bleeding?" My voice was small and tentative.

There was a sound of tape being pulled off and then Grant cleared his throat. "It stopped. Started healing, too." He looked up at me, surprise painted across his face. "That's weird."

I didn't take my eyes off the road this time. "Yeah. Yeah, it's weird."

A sign advertising a gas station at the next exit caught my eye. I flipped the headlights on and off a few times. Andy gave me the thumbs up and turned on his blinker. We exited the highway and pulled up to a gas pump. I turned off the car and sat back in the seat, allowing my frayed nerves to settle a bit. I was going to need strength for this next part.

The back door opened and closed, and Grant swiped his card into the reader and started filling up the tank. I looked over at the pump next to us and saw Andy doing the same. I pushed open the door and leaned against it to open it, nearly falling out of the seat as I did so. The morning had worn me out more than I realized.

Grant was there, his hands on my arm, helping me up. "Whoa, there. Take it slow."

"I'm fine." I stood up and closed the door, dropping his keys into his hand. "I'm going to go in and use the bathroom."

"Um, yeah. You sure you're good to walk?"

I nodded, not meeting his gaze. "I'll grab a new shirt for you while I'm in there." I walked toward the glass doors and pulled one open, relishing the warmth that spilled out from the inside. An old woman sat behind the counter, gnawing on a piece of breakfast pizza and watching an old soap opera on her tablet. She barely glanced up from it when I entered.

"Um, excuse me? Where are your restrooms?"

She didn't look up but pointed with a greasy finger to the back of the store near the cold soda and beer.

"Thanks," I mumbled, making my way through the shelves of chips, candy, and aspirin. The sickening sweet smell of donuts in the glass counter made my stomach turn as I passed. I yanked open the door to the ladies' room and pulled it closed behind me, turning the silver lock with a click. The restroom had seen better days, but at least it was clean. I used the bathroom and then pulled off a huge wad of paper towels. I ran them under the hot water then wiped my face and neck. It felt good to be clean and now that we were out of Culvers Grove, everything felt better in general. My stomach roiled now, but for a different reason. I stared at myself in the mirror. *You have to do this. There's no other choice.* I nodded, ignoring the tears that welled up in my eyes. I unlocked the door and met Evie standing in the small hallway near a mop propped up in a bucket of filthy gray water. She was dancing from foot to foot and almost knocked me over as she sprinted into the bathroom.

"Tristan's in the men's room and Andy's getting something to eat," she said before the door slammed behind her.

I wandered out into the store and up toward the front corner where some T-shirts were hanging. I moved them to the side one by one, the metal hangers ringing as they slid across the bar. I got to the end of the mediums and realized I hadn't really looked at any of them. I shook my head and tried to wade out of the numbness that was taking over. Plucking a green shirt from the rack, I went up to the counter and paid for it.

Grant was still outside, cleaning his windows with the squeegee and knocking the dirty snow from the wheel wells. He looked up as I approached.

"Hey, you did a good job driving us out of there." He walked over and wrapped an arm around me, bending down to kiss the top of my head. "I'm proud of you."

"Here," I said, pulling away from his grasp and shoving the T-shirt out at him.

"Thanks." He took it and spread it out in front of him, holding it up to read what was printed on the front. A chuckle escaped him and he looked over at me. "Clever." He raised an eye and then shook off his coat, laying it on the hood of his car.

I bit my bottom lip, my eyes going straight to the bloodstain on his shirt.

Grant saw me looking and his face softened. "It's better, Marissa. Really. Look, I'm fine now." He pulled up the hem of his shirt and tore away the bandage. There were scratches on his stomach, but they were almost completely healed over and there was no redness around them. "Like it never happened," he said. He threw the bandage in the garbage can and then took his shirt off and threw it in as well. Gooseflesh rose up on his arms and back and he shivered before pulling the green shirt on.

"What's the plan, Anderson?" Andy came out of the gas station with three slices of breakfast pizza balanced in one hand and an enormous vat of soda in the other. A plastic bag full of sodas, chips, and granola bars hung from the crook of his elbow. He walked over to the truck and stood staring at the door, until Tristan came to his rescue and held the soda, while Andy put the bag on the seat.

Evie walked up next to me. "Nice shirt," she quipped, nodding in Grant's direction.

I swallowed. "We have to go to the quarry."

My statement was met with silence. Then everyone started talking at once.

"No way, Anderson."

"What good will that do?"

"I don't think that's a good idea."

"We just got out of there. Why do you want to go right back in?"

When they stopped talking, I took a deep breath. "Whatever is below the courthouse has my dad and half of my family. It probably has my grandma now, too." I sighed. "I have to help."

"If you want to go, I'll go with you," Evie said. Her voice was soft, but her green eyes blazed.

"Me, too," Tristan said. He nodded and placed a hand on my shoulder.

"Agrlubsfbl."

We all turned to look at Andy.

He stopped chewing and swallowed. "I said that I'm in, too."

"So, let's get going," Grant said. He pulled the nozzle from the gas tank and replaced the cap.

My stomach churned and tears burned the back of my eyes. "Not you," I whispered.

Grant froze and looked up at me. "What?"

"Not you." I cleared my throat and took a deep breath. "None of us are hurt, we can handle it better. We get sick. If you go back in, you'll bleed to death. You have to go back to school. Get away from all of this." I swept my hand in a large arc, my voice barely containing its tremor.

"I'll be fine," Grant said. He came forward and took my hand in his.

I yanked it back. "I don't want you here. This is too hard and I can't do it anymore."

"Don't do this, Marissa." Grant dropped his voice, his eyes searching mine. "Please."

I closed my eyes. When I opened them, I stared right into Grant's eyes. "I don't want to be with you. Whatever this is, or was, it's over."

"You don't mean that."

"Andy, I'm ready to go." I turned and walked toward the truck, the tears I had been holding back began pouring out and running down my cheeks. Yanking the door open, I climbed in and sat, folding myself down over my middle.

The other door opened and I felt someone slide in next to me.

"Marissa, are you sure about this?" Tristan grabbed my hand and held it.

I nodded, biting back another sob.

"You didn't think he'd leave unless you broke up with him."

I nodded again.

The door opened and Andy and Evie got into the truck, sandwiching Tristan and me between them. The truck roared to life and Andy put it in gear.

"Back to Culvers Grove?" he asked.

I nodded for the third time.

As we left the parking lot, I turned to look through the back window.

Grant stood, leaning against his car, his hands shoved deep in his pockets, the green T-shirt with *I Survived the Great Corn Maze of Culvers Grove, Missouri* in stark contrast to his blue car. He looked up at me as we turned onto the entrance ramp, his eyes following the truck until we dropped out of sight.

"That was harsh, Anderson." Andy shifted, keeping the truck in low as he crawled along the snowy highway. A snowplow cleared the westbound lanes, its orange lights reflecting off the snow in the median between us.

"Shut up." I sniffed and Tristan handed me a tissue.

"We all know he was getting it worse than any of us. He can't come back inside the wall." Evie leaned around me to look at Andy. "Be nice."

My phone buzzed. I pulled it out and looked down.

Did you think it would be that easy?

My stomach twisting, I turned to look behind us. Grant's car flipped its lights at me.

"He's following us."

Andy glanced up in his rearview.

I called Grant. "What are you doing?" I asked when he picked up.

"You didn't mean it."

"Fine. I didn't mean it. But, I did mean it when I said you can't come back in. You saw what happened last time."

"I'm willing to take my chances."

I covered the phone and looked over at Andy. "He won't leave."

"He can't go back in," Tristan said. "He's too hurt."

"What do I do?" I asked, my voice high pitched with worry.

Andy glanced in his rearview again. "You're sure you don't want him to come, right?"

"He can't," I said.

"Hold on." With a flick of his wrist, Andy downshifted and hit his brakes, the truck shuddering and the rear end sliding toward the shoulder.

"What are you doing?" I gripped the dashboard, almost dropping my phone.

Andy got control of the truck. "Evasive maneuver. Hand me your phone."

I looked behind us again. Grant's car sat sideways in the ditch, the passenger side wedged against the snowbank.

"Andy!" I groaned.

Andy snatched the phone from my hand. "You okay, bro?" He smiled at whatever Grant's response was and then looked over at me. "He's not mad at *you* anymore." He winked. "Yeah, man. Sorry about that. Must've hit some black ice. Flag down the plow when it comes back your way." He handed the phone to me and I stared at him, mouth open.

Tristan hid a chuckle behind his hand.

"Do you actually condone this behavior?" I asked Tristan as I placed the phone to my ear. "Hey, Grant."

"Your friend owes me a mirror. Sheared right off the side."

"I'm sorry."

He chuckled. "I know. I'm sorry, too. Sorry I was so stubborn." He dropped his voice. "Listen, Marissa. I love you and I'll be here for you when you need me."

He chuckled again. "Well, I'll be here until the plow pulls me out, but you know what I mean."

"Love you, too," I whispered.

The call disconnected and I stared at the white out in front of us. The snow started falling again as we crossed over the barrier.

CHAPTER 10

The air seemed thicker here somehow. Gray clouds hung low in the sky, bearing down on us as we made our way through the snow to the entrance to the quarry. The morning squall had been intense, but short-lived, only dropping another half inch or so of snow on the twelve plus already on the ground. We'd parked Andy's truck in a small lot near the driveway and changed into boots and heavy coats before heading out. He and Tristan both carried backpacks weighed down with equipment for our trip into the cave. Tristan had charged his phone on the way out and was now furiously scrolling through screens. Evie guided him with a hand on his elbow.

"I can't find anything. Just the map of the one part of the caves we already went through." He closed his phone and put it in his pocket with a sigh. "That means we're going in blind. I don't like it."

I forged ahead, trying to convey confidence with the way I held my shoulders. An article I read once said that ninety-two percent of people's conversations take place through nonverbal communication, and holding your shoulders square and your neck extended portrayed self-confidence. Of course, that was a stance easier to accomplish when you weren't walking through a foot of snow. After tripping for the tenth time, I gave up the illusion of confidence and settled for remaining upright.

"Why is the gate open?"

Evie's voice brought us all up short. We stood shoulder to shoulder in the snow, our eyes locked on the gate. Made of heavy steel, capped with rolls of barbed wire, and standing nine feet in the air, the gates to the Loroxco Mining Company were usually a formidable aspect of the landscape. Now, though, they had been reduced to a pile of twisted metal.

"Someone wanted in there really badly," Evie said.

"Huh uh." Andy walked over to the metal and pointed. "The way this is laying here, someone wanted *out* really badly."

A shiver wound its way through me, turning my blood to icicles. "Who did this?"

Andy picked up a piece of the lock plate and shrugged.

"We're still going in, right?" I looked around at the group. "I mean, we don't know what happened here."

Evie placed her hand on my arm. "Calm down, St. Louis. We're still going in. We'll find your dad." She nodded and I moved my head up and down, mirroring her. "Do you get anything here?" Casting her eyes down the long driveway, she squinted. "I think I see a disturbance, but…" she glanced back at me, "well, you know."

I concentrated on the small metal building in the distance. It sat nestled between two enormous piles of gravel and a gargantuan earthmover perched near the edge of the excavation location. Something pulled at me from the building. "This way," I said, moving my unwilling feet down the driveway. I let out the breath I had been holding when I heard the snow crunching behind me as my friends followed.

As we approached, the sky descended again. Something my grandma used to say flitted through my mind. *If the clouds get any lower, I'll be able to reach up and grab one.* I shook my head. The thought of grabbing hold of one used to fascinate me as a small child. I spent hours lying in the grass in our backyard, reaching my hand out toward the little balls of fluff racing across the sky. Those were happy clouds, though.

I glanced up. These clouds would probably coat my hand.

Like smoke. Black smoke.

Images flashed through my mind. Jeff, Evie's dad, sitting across from her in the hospital room, the black smoke curling around his ankles. Beth pulled back to the ground, the black smoke caressing her legs. The black smoke figure jettisoning out of Mary's ghost at the Weeping Bridge. My dad, alone and scared, as the black smoke approached, getting closer. I swallowed and picked up my pace.

The building was little more than a trailer with a three-step stoop leading up to the door. It was open, the door moving back and forth lazily. My foot was on the first step when I felt a hand on my shoulder.

"This doesn't feel right." Andy shook his head and held up a heavy metal flashlight. "At least let me go first?"

I acquiesced and moved to the side to allow him to pass. "I don't feel much here. I mean, I don't think there are any spirits."

He glanced back at me. "It's not the dead I'm worried about." Andy disappeared inside and I followed.

The second I stepped inside, I threw my hand over my mouth and nose. My eyes teared up and I felt bile rising. "What *is* that?"

Andy turned watering eyes in my direction. He shrugged, turned a shade of green and dashed past me through the open door.

I could hear him retching over the railing as I made my way around the desk. There, I found the source of the smell. The sides of my mouth turned downward as I grabbed a newspaper off the desk and reached down to wrap the rotting corpse of a raccoon in the paper. I held it out in front of me and picked my way out the door, descending the steps and walking over to the side of the driveway.

"Oh my gosh! What is that?" Tristan held his sleeve over his mouth.

My stomach churning, I placed the newspaper on the ground. I used my feet to shovel a thick covering of snow onto the dead animal. Then, I stood up and considered my gloves for a minute.

"Burn them!" Andy yelled from the stoop before throwing up again.

I pulled them off carefully and tossed them on the ground.

"Here," Tristan said, offering me a bottle of hand sanitizer before stepping away again.

I used half the bottle and washed down my hands, wrists, and for good measure, wiped some across my mouth and nose, wincing as the alcohol burned. When I was finished, I walked over to the building, taking the clean pair of gloves Tristan held out to me.

"Thanks," I mumbled. I climbed the steps.

"Where are you going, Anderson?"

"I'm going to open a window. It should be better in a few minutes." Inside, I opened two windows on opposite sides of the room, allowing the icy wind to churn through, carrying out the scent of decay. In a doored cabinet, I found a bottle of room spray and gave it a couple shots into the air.

Andy poked his head through the door. "All better?"

I nodded. "I think so."

Evie appeared beside Andy, her brows knit with worry. "Tristan's going to stay outside and keep watch." She elbowed past Andy and stood in the middle of the room. "You take the papers on the desk, and Andy, you see if you can get the surveillance equipment running." She pointed to the cabinet where two television screens stared blankly out from the shelf.

Andy nodded and moved over to the cabinet while I descended on the desk, shuffling through the papers coating its surface. Evie disappeared into the smaller room and turned on the light, revealing shelves of paperwork. I rifled through a pile on the corner of the desk, straightening the papers as I uncovered a logbook.

"You know, you don't have to clean up after them," Evie quipped as she came out of the small room. "Nothing in there. How's the camera?"

Andy glanced up at her. "I got into the feeds. Playing them back now."

I grabbed the book and walked across the room to look at the screens over his shoulder.

"That feed is from a camera probably mounted right above us, pointed that way." He jutted a thumb to his left, toward the quarry. "The other one is from the driveway. See the gate?"

I nodded. "How far back did you go?"

He squinted. "This is from last night. They must only keep the feeds for twenty-four hours. This is all they have on the computer."

I watched the snow begin to fall on the grainy black and white screen.

"What was that?" Evie took a breath in.

Andy stopped and rewound the camera from the top of the trailer. When it played back again, I could see what she was talking about.

"That mist, there," I pointed. "Is that what you saw?"

She nodded, her arms folded across her chest.

We watched as the mist floated near an opening in the side of the rock. Then, it wound its way up toward the trailer, snaking through the snowflakes. I swallowed. As it got nearer, it started to take on the shape of a person. It bore down on the trailer and then moved out of frame.

"Where did it go?" I whispered.

Andy shrugged.

We leaned in to stare at the screen and jumped when the camera shook.

"What was that?" Evie asked. The dark circles under her eyes deepened.

"My guess is the door slamming open or closed. Hard enough to shake the trailer." He tilted his head. "That was around eleven last night."

"Look!" Evie pointed at the second screen. Headlights came into view and then a pickup truck barreled through, fishtailing as its tires lost tread in the thickening blanket of snow. The angle of the shot obscured the driver's face, but his hands were gripping the steering wheel tightly.

"He's not going to stop," Andy commented.

As if in response, the truck picked up speed and crashed through the gate, tearing off the front metal plate and shredding the sides of the truck with the metal. The truck disappeared off frame and then both cameras were filled with shots of falling snow. The flakes were thick and pretty soon, there was nothing more to see but the almost white-out of the night before. Andy fast-forwarded through the remaining recording, but nothing else happened until we arrived.

He shrugged and turned off the monitors. "Now what?"

I looked down at the book in my hand. Turning to the first page, I read several entries consisting of mundane things like 10:02 p.m. October 12, stray dog on property - Animal Control called. 11:06 p.m. November 6, unauthorized vehicle on premises. I flipped through more pages. "Look at this." I angled the book so that they could see it and read out loud. "December 15, 9:02 p.m. Trailer shaking. December 15 10:15 p.m. Heard children laughing outside. Investigated, but found nothing." I looked up at my friends.

"His handwriting got messier," Evie commented.

"He was scared."

I turned the page. "December 27, 10:18 p.m. Unauthorized person at the door. Notified him that I had a firearm and that he was to leave. Smoke under door. Opened door to find nothing. Then, 11:04 p.m. December 27. Left to go home. Illness." I flipped through several entries of illness and then put my finger on the last page. "This is last night. Listen. 9:52 p.m. Trailer shaking. 9:58 p.m. Knocking on door. 10:02 p.m. Child singing. 10:13 p.m. Smoke filled up trailer. 10:26 p.m. Footsteps on stairs. Voices all around the trailer. 10:42 p.m. The voices. Someone's out there. Phone not working. No way to contact police."

"Is that it?" Evie asked.

I shook my head. "There's one more." I ran my finger down the page to the last shaky entry. Taking a deep breath, I read the words. "10:59 p.m. Don't know what's going on. The voices. Banging on the windows and doors. There are so many of them. Going to make a run for it. Tell my family I love them." There was a long shaky line as the "m" was dragged down to the bottom of the page.

I closed the logbook and handed it to Evie. None of us spoke for a full minute.

"You still want to go in there?" Evie whispered finally.

Tears stung my eyes. I bit my lip. "I-I have to."

CHAPTER 11

"In there, huh?" Andy wiped the back of his hand across his mouth. He'd thrown up twice during the long walk down the rock ramp to the bottom of the quarry.

I nodded, my jaw set. My heart was still racing from the argument that had taken place back up at the trailer. When we came out, Tristan had all of the equipment from the backpacks laid out and he was doing an inventory.

"I'm going alone," I stated calmly.

The group had looked at me as if I'd lost my mind.

"No way, Anderson."

Tristan began packing up the stuff. "Not even an option."

"Look at all of you!" I shouted, my voice echoing in the empty space. "You're all sick! Andy can't stop throwing up, Evie looks like death warmed over, and you haven't been able to eat anything all day!" My voice amped up as my throat constricted around my tears. "You have to get out of here. Out of this town."

Tristan stood with his hands on his hips. "You done?"

I blinked and nodded.

He took a step forward and grabbed my hand in his. "Marissa Anderson, you are our friend. You're family and your dad is family. We're not leaving you." His eyes peered into mine, unwavering. "This is *our* deal, too."

Andy reached over and placed a hand on my shoulder. "You're my troop, fam."

A smile escaped and I breathed out. "Fine. Evie?"

She nodded, too, her arms wrapped around her middle. "You know how I feel, St. Louis."

I nodded and led the way down into the quarry, the fear inside me taking hold with icy fingers the further down we got. Now that we stood at the entrance to the caves, I allowed the fear to take over. It somehow gave me strength and I steeled myself for the journey.

"When we get in there, no one breaks off from the group, understand?" Andy's voice was resigned. "We go in together, and we stay together."

Tristan handed out flashlights. "I don't have service down here, so there won't be any way to communicate if we lose someone."

My stomach flopped as I took the flashlight he gave me. I turned to look at the yawning black rip in the rock wall. The floor was about three feet above the ground and the opening was only a couple of feet across. It spread up through the rock, ending in a crack that ran up to the sky. I swallowed and flipped the light on. The beam disappeared into the blackness. Choking down the emotion crashing down on my soul, I put my hands on the sides of the rock and pulled myself up through the opening.

The second I stepped into the tunnel, silence took over all my senses. I squinted, trying to peer down the opening as I made my way along, scooting my feet the way Tristan had told us as we walked down the ramp. He said that we didn't want to step down into open space if a cavern happened to open up under us. I gulped and kept going.

My friends climbed in behind me, making their way single file through the narrow space. As Andy stood up, he blocked out the daylight and I took a sharp breath in, closing my eyes for a second as my fear of dying underground froze me to the spot. I took another deep breath and thought of my dad. His face came into focus in my mind's eye. My chest heaved with a choked sob as his image smiled, his eyes laughing. I opened my eyes and shuffled along, the beam of light cutting through the darkness.

"How far do you think we'll have to go?" Evie breathed.

"We're about five miles outside of town here," Tristan said.

The thought of traveling that far under the earth terrified me. *There's no other way.* I kept going, driving myself forward through sheer force of will. Soon, the tunnel widened and we were able to walk two-by-two. Evie's shoulder brushed mine as we walked.

"Are you scared?" she whispered.

I nodded, and then realized she couldn't see me. "Yeah. Terrified."

"Me, too."

We walked for another fifteen minutes before the cave opened up again. Our flashlight beams combined in the huge space, lighting up stalactites hanging from the ceiling. Droplets of water fell to the floor, landing on the limestone and creating slick, wet rivulets of stone.

"Check that out," Andy said, shining his light on the wall opposite of where we were standing. The cave went off in two directions from here. He crossed the room and stood, peering into the darkness of one tunnel and then the other.

"Which way?" I asked.

He turned and shrugged. "No idea. They both look the same."

"We could…" I began.

Tristan cut me off. "If you say what I think you're going to say, I swear I will disown you." He walked over to join Andy. They stood with their backs to Evie and me, their heads together as they considered their options.

"Speak up already," I grumbled.

Andy turned. "He says we have to split up."

Tristan whirled around. "I did not!"

"Come on," Andy said, bumping Tristan's shoulder with his. "Do you really see any other way?"

"Absolutely not. We don't have a map. We don't know where either of these go, and if we get into trouble…" His voice faded off and he shone his flashlight in my face.

"Hey!" I threw my hand up to shield my eyes.

"What was that face?" he asked.

"What are you talking about? And quit shining that in my eyes!"

"I saw it, too. You heard something." Andy's face was drawn tight.

I shook my head. "I, um, I thought I heard something from down there." I gestured to the tunnel on the right and let my hand flop back to my side.

"What? What did you hear?"

I shook my head again. "It's stupid."

"Anderson."

"Fine. I thought I heard someone walking, but it's stopped now and we can keep going."

Evie eyed me and then walked over to the tunnel. She leaned forward then shook her head. "I can't see anything."

"See? It's fine." My stomach churned. I *had* heard someone walking, but there was no way anyone would be down here in the caves. It was my fear taking over and if we were going to save my dad, I couldn't let it chase me out of the cave. "Let's keep going, please?"

Tristan started coughing, and this time, it doubled him over where he stood. Andy supported him as he coughed, the sound filling up the entire room. I grabbed a bottle of water from my bag and twisted the cap off. He took it gratefully and took two long drinks, his coughing fit finally abating. Ripping the straps from his shoulders, he let the backpack fall to the ground and he followed, sitting down with a grunt.

"Are you okay?" I asked.

He held up a hand and nodded. "Fine," he gasped, drawing shallow breaths.

"The coughing will start again if he breathes too deeply," Andy said. "He'll be fine in a minute."

Tristan patted Andy's hand and sat, breathing shallowly. The cavern grew quiet as we all watched him.

I heard a noise from the tunnel and swung my light that way. *Nothing. Get hold of yourself.* Then, I heard it again. A wet, scraping sound. From the other tunnel. I jerked my light around and held my breath as I listened to the sound. *Footsteps.* They were getting closer, and there were more than one of them.

"We have to go," I said as calmly as I could. "We have to get out of here, now. Tristan, can you walk?"

He nodded and stood up. Andy grabbed the strap of his bag and pulled it to his chest, so he was wearing a backpack on his back and one on his front. Evie put her arm around Tristan's middle. He threw his arm around her shoulders and nodded again.

Dread made my breathing shallow and I felt my head begin to spin. I forced myself to take a deep breath. "Come on." I shone the flashlight across the room to the opening we'd come through a few minutes before. "This way."

"Are you sure?" Evie asked as she came up next to me. "You don't want to go down the other tunnel?"

"Something's coming from each of them," I whispered. As I turned my flashlight, it caught Tristan's face. His eyes were watery and wide. He looked more scared than I'd ever seen him. I let Evie and Tristan head down the tunnel first and grabbed at Andy's hand.

Before we left the cavern, I swung my flashlight behind me, bathing the space in the cool glow. From the two tunnels, shapes emerged. I tilted my head, unsure of what I was seeing at first. Then horror gripped me as I realized what was happening again.

They were people.

A lot of them. Pouring from the openings, they dragged their bodies from the tunnels, hollow eyes set on the opposite wall where I was standing.

"Time to go, Anderson," Andy said, pulling me from the sight.

The sloshing sound of them moving across the stone followed me as we turned and ran.

CHAPTER 12

Halfway up the ramp away from the tunnel, my legs finally gave out. I sat down heavily in the snow, my chest rising and falling as I gasped for air.

Evie stopped. Her arm was still around Tristan's middle. "St. Louis, we can't stop now."

"I know," I panted. I glanced up at the rim of the giant hole cut from the ground.

Andy came up behind me and sank down to his knees. "They're still coming."

I closed my eyes. "You can see them?"

"Yeah." He retched and then cleared his throat. "I can see them."

"They're a lot stronger now," Evie said. "I can see them, too."

I opened my eyes and looked down. The figures continued to pour out from the tunnel opening, falling over one another as they spilled out onto the ground.

"Hey," I whispered, "isn't that..." My throat closed up.

"It's Red," Andy confirmed.

I watched as his eyes stared vacantly up the rise and he began shuffling toward us, the blood congealing around the edge of his helmet. "I don't understand. When we left, he was fine. He was sitting on the picnic table outside the cafeteria. We put him to...sleep again."

Andy wiped at his mouth with a snow-covered glove. "Something woke him up." He grunted as he stood up, using the rock face to his left to steady himself on his feet. "Come on, Anderson," he said, grabbing my arm, "We have to get out of here." He pulled, but there was no strength in his grasp and my arm slid from his hands.

It fell limply against my side. I sat there, my stringy hair falling in my face. Everything in my body hurt. I looked up at the rim again. I nodded. *I got them into this. It's my responsibility to get them out.* Standing up, I wavered for a moment on legs filled with jelly.

"Give me your keys." I held a gloved hand out toward Andy.

He furrowed his brow.

"Come on. I'm the least sick of all of us. I'll go ahead and get the truck. I'll meet you by the trailer."

"Your color's off," Evie commented. She shuffled Tristan's body against her hip and started walking uphill again.

Andy's keys jangled into my palm. I put them in my pocket and began walking.

"I thought you couldn't see those anymore," I mumbled as I walked past them on the narrow ledge.

"No, I mean your color's off. We can all see that."

I ignored her comment and peered ahead at the rim. We had almost a quarter mile to go before we reached the top. Then, another quarter mile to get the truck. My stomach churned. Suddenly, I remembered something my mom told me once. We had been walking around the neighborhood one day after school. When she found out she was sick, she changed everything about the way she ate and exercised. The evening walks had become something she never missed, even though her pace got slower and more uneven with each passing day. That evening, she grimaced as we turned the corner under the streetlights.

"Do you want to go back home?" I asked.

She shook her head, breathing hard. "No, I need to make it around the block."

I watched her fight through the pain, as she took a few more steps. I fell into pace beside her.

"I don't know how you do it," I said.

Mom looked at me and chuckled. "You sound like your grandmother."

"How do you keep walking when it hurts so much?"

Her eyes softened. "I can take one step. That's all I think about. I don't think about all of the other steps I'll need to take to get around the block. I only think about the next step. Then, when I've done that, I start thinking about the next one."

I caught a whiff of lavender on the breeze and closed my eyes, relishing the scent. Then, I shook my head and stared up at the rim of the quarry again. *Don't think about making it up there.* I focused on a spot about fifty steps ahead. *You can make it there.* I forced my feet to move, even though they felt like they were weighted down with concrete. One step, then another. Just like my mom.

When I made it to the first goal, I glanced behind me. Evie and Tristan had pulled ahead of Andy, who was practically crawling at this point. Further down, the horde of spirits moved slowly, but relentlessly. I gulped and turned around again, focusing on a spot farther up. I could feel the pull the group of ghosts was having on my soul and I fought against it. *You can't stop now.*

Four more times, I focused on the steps directly in front of me, and when my head finally popped over the side, I almost wept with joy. I turned to my friends. "I made it!" I yelled. My cry died in my throat as I peered over the side at them. Evie and Tristan were still a hundred feet behind, limping along, holding one another up. Andy had fallen further back, his body hunched over as he shuffled slowly. He ran a hand along the rock wall on his side, the other held over his mouth. My heart stopped. The spirits were only yards behind him now. From that vantage point, I noticed something I hadn't before: a black cloud of smoke winding in and out of the group, snaking along their feet and bodies, urging them forward up the ramp.

No! I shook my head. *This can't be happening!* I looked over my shoulder. The truck was still at the gate. There was no way I could reach it and get it back here in time. Even if I had the strength to get back down the ramp to Andy, there was no way I could reach him before the horde did. Icy tendrils of fear ran through my arms and legs. I choked on a sob. "Andy!"

He looked up at me then, his eyes calm. A smile cracked his face and he shrugged. He nodded toward Evie and Tristan and I knew what I had to do. Tears began to cloud my vision as I stepped back over the edge and began the descent. Evie glanced up at me as I reached them and took Tristan's other arm around my shoulders. She squinted at me and nodded her head toward Andy. I swallowed and shook my head in a small movement. Tears filled her eyes and she looked down, intent on the ground in front of us.

Step by step, we fought our way to the top again, collapsing in a heap when we reached the rim. Tristan faded in and out of consciousness, his head lolling to his chest. His breathing was labored and a sick rattling sound came from his throat.

Evie looked up at me. "He's really sick."

I nodded, the growing hopelessness of the situation pressing down on me. I wanted to close my eyes, to hunker down and make believe this was all a bad dream. *No dice, Marissa. You passed up that delusion about six ghosts ago.* I shook my head and looked over the edge. Andy was still moving, but barely. Behind him, the spirits bore down on him, only yards away now. Emotion tore at my soul, threatening to bury me in sadness. I watched as the smoke twisted away from the group and snaked along the ground toward my friend.

"No!" I yelled, but the sound came out a ragged whisper from my tortured throat. I tried to get up, to stand, but there was no more juice left in me. I was spent. Completely and utterly spent.

This was how it was going to end. I would watch as the monsters took my friends one by one before finally taking me. I wondered if it would hurt. Staring down at Andy, my heart broke. Tears wound down my cheeks, burning the chapped skin. I tried to get up again, but my legs failed me. *I can't let him be alone!* That one thought catapulted me into a half crouch, the muscles in my legs shaking with the effort.

Then I felt a hand on my shoulder. It pressed down. I lost my footing and fell back into the snow bank next to Evie and Tristan.

"Someone order a hero?"

Grant's voice shot through me like an arrow. I looked up into his face as it smiled down at me. *Now, I'm dreaming.* I reached up with a gloved hand and placed it on his cheek.

"I-I don't understand."

He smiled. "You get Evie and Tristan to my car. It's right in front of the trailer." He glanced over the rim of the quarry. "I guess I'm going to go save him." He rolled his eyes and then grimaced. Blood was beginning to soak through the green T-shirt he wore, creating a dot of brown on the hem.

"You're hurt."

He looked down. "I'll be fine." He leaned down and kissed me on the forehead. "You get them to the car. I'll take care of the rest." With that, he stood up and started jogging down the ramp. "Hey, Andy, you owe me a side mirror!"

CHAPTER 13

I wiped away the condensation on the car window and peered through it, willing Andy and Grant to come around the corner of the trailer. Evie and Tristan sat in the back, their breath coming in short blasts as they panted from the effort of getting to Grant's car.

"They'll be safe, St. Louis," Evie said, her voice cracking.

I nodded, my eyes not leaving the space between the trailer and the gravel pile. "Maybe I should go out there."

"Right. You'd be so much help."

I glanced back at her, a snarky comment on my lips. It withered away when I saw the dark circles under her eyes. Tristan's head was back, resting against the headrest as he struggled to breathe.

"Is he going to be okay?" she asked, unzipping her coat to spread it over them both.

I nodded. "We're all going to be okay." I wished I thought it was true. Turning my attention back to the trailer, a strangled cry built up from my core. "There they are!"

Grant was practically carrying Andy, the snow hindering their progress. I opened the door and put my legs out.

"Stay in the car!" Grant called out.

I yanked my legs back in, fear building inside me as I saw Red's spirit come into view. He was only steps behind them. My throat constricted. I turned to Evie.

"Open the door!"

She shoved Tristan over behind the driver's seat and then pushed the back door open with her foot. My heart raced as Grant and Andy crossed the open space to the car.

He deposited Andy in the backseat and slammed the door closed. I shut my door and stared out at Red's ghost as it moved toward the car. Transfixed by his hollow eyes, my chest burned with emotion.

"But, we saved you," I whispered.

Grant fell into the driver's seat and started the car, the engine grinding for a heart-stopping split second before catching and roaring to life. Heat poured from the vents, blowing tendrils of my hair from my cheek.

Red's eyes reached out to me, pulling me toward him. He opened his mouth and a black cloud of smoke shot out, smacking against the window. I jumped back and cried out, my hand flying to my face as the smoke dripped down the window, leaving an oily coating behind.

"Time to go," Grant said. He put the car in gear and turned it around, hitting the gas and fishtailing as we sped past the trailer, the horde of spirits trailing us onto the driveway.

I turned to look out the back window. Red opened his mouth again, the cloud of smoke shooting out and hitting the car. It shuddered and Grant glanced up in the rearview mirror. He set his jaw, his knuckles turning white as he gripped the steering wheel. The car churned up snow as it sped toward the shattered gate.

"St. Louis!"

I spun around again and saw a tendril of smoke working its way through the window, spinning as it threaded down toward Andy. I turned around in my seat and grabbed at it, crying out as it slid through my fingers like liquid fire. It was like trying to hold onto water, though, and I watched with horror as it spun toward Andy's open mouth.

"No!" I made one last grab for it as it hesitated. It slid through my fingers again and shot into Andy's mouth.

The second it was in, Andy bolted upright, his eyes and mouth open wide. Fear coated his features. He sucked a huge breath in, pulling the tendril into him, and then he froze. A tear escaped from his eye and wound its way down his cheek.

Evie had turned sideways in the seat, pressing her back into Tristan, her arms held wide in a protective stance. "Andy?" Her voice was small.

"Stop the car," I said. My voice was strong.

Grant glanced over at me, his eyes questioning.

I nodded. "Stop the car."

I felt the car slow down and then stop. I turned my attention back to Andy. The tail of the smoke trail was on his chin and I made a mad grab at it. *You will not take my friend!* I closed my eyes, concentrating on the spark inside me. I fed it, allowed it to grow to an ember, igniting the tinder of anger surrounding my heart. Heat spread through me and I felt the tail of the smoke solidify in my fingers. It became an entity, a *thing*. I clamped down on it and pulled.

When I opened my eyes, I saw the smoke spread like taffy from my hands to Andy's mouth. I pulled at it, willing it to release its hold on my friend. I let the anger grow, festering inside like a wound. The wound my mother left when she died. The wound my dad left when he was taken away. The wounds of trying to help everyone but helping no one and making it worse in the process. I opened myself up, allowing the anger to overtake me.

Suddenly, the smoke stopped pulling away from me, instead rising up between us almost like a question mark. Yellow light spread from my fingertips, spiraling along the smoke toward Andy. As it did, a red light spread from Andy's side, rising along the trail. The strings of light met in the middle, intermingling in an orange glow that spun around the smoke. Evie gasped as the tendril hesitated for a moment and then shot toward me, out of Andy's mouth and into my chest, spreading like a virus, wrapping around my body. I welcomed it as it wound around me like a boa constrictor. It coated me with a viscous substance that burned and made it hard to breathe.

"Marissa?" Grant reached his hand out to me.

I shook my head. "Don't. Touch. Me." The words were clipped. Each breath I took hurt and I felt the smoke gaining strength from my core.

Grant drew his hand back. He looked back at Andy.

"Drive," Andy said, wiping the tear from his cheek. "We have to get out of town. *Now.*"

Grant nodded and put the car in gear. He cast a worried glance in my direction as I turned to face the front of the car. I felt the smoke tugging at me, trying to find a way inside. I blocked it at every turn, but it was taking all of the energy I had. I concentrated on the road ahead.

You only have to make it to the end of the driveway. I nodded to myself. My feet started to tingle and I wiggled my toes inside my boots. We got to Andy's truck and Grant stopped the car, got out and popped the trunk. He followed Andy's directions and pulled out several bags from the toolbox, throwing them in the truck. He closed the door and raced back into the car.

I noticed that the bloodstain on his shirt had spread. Ugly blotches covered the material. I swallowed, the momentary lapse in my attention allowing the smoke to tighten its crushing grip. I fought against it, keeping the pain at bay. It pulled at me, though, and I felt hopelessness spread through my heart. *It's going to win. It's going to take everyone in this town. The dead and the living.* I heard the words as they slid around my mind, whispered in a whiny drone, like a mosquito buzzing near my ear.

I shook my head and stared out the windshield as Grant turned the car onto the main road. It had been cleared and we picked up speed on our way to the highway.

"Is she breathing?"

"Anderson? Are you still with us?"

"Grant, hurry."

I heard my friends, but I was past the point of communication. The smoke left welts in its wake as it twisted around my middle, burning the skin. I felt tears falling from my eyes but could do nothing to stop them. Every fiber of my being was concentrated on holding the smoke at bay. At keeping it from my friends. I held onto it and welcomed the pain, my chest rising and falling with the labored breathing as the pain and anger melded together, searing my flesh.

Then I was falling. My vision grew blurry around the edges and I felt myself draining faster than I had ever experienced before. From somewhere out of the darkness that was overtaking me, I heard a voice. It was outside. No. Inside. Madness rushed in on me. *If you let it in, the pain will stop. Everything will stop. No more hurt. No more pain. No more anger.* I hesitated, my guard dropping for a moment as I considered its offer.

The smoke saw its opening. It lunged at my chest again and again, knocking against my ribcage with a thundering pressure. My heart felt like it was going to explode and my lungs burned with the effort of breathing. The smoke pressed down on my chest, driving out the need for air, the need for anything of this world. My eyes rolled wildly around in their sockets as I struggled against it, rallying everything in my being to shove back against its relentless onslaught.

It was a losing battle, though.

I had nothing left to give. The pain was suddenly gone and with it, the anger faded as well. I was only a shell, a vessel for the smoke. I had nothing left to give. I closed my eyes and gave up.

A second later, something slammed into me with the force of a truck. I sat up, sucking a giant breath into my lungs. Everything hurt, but somehow, that was comforting. Something about the hurt let me know I was still connected, still viable. Still alive. I sucked breath after breath into my battered lungs, relishing the air as it filled my insides, driving out the last vestiges of the nightmare.

"Marissa?"

Grant's voice reached me and I swung my head over to look at him, my chest rising and falling. The car was stopped along the shoulder of an exit ramp. The sun shone down on the snow, blinding me for a moment as I climbed out of the darkness.

"Marissa?" Grant said again. This time, he reached out, cupping my face in gentle hands. They shook as he gazed into my eyes.

"W-what happened?" My throat was shredded and the words came out a raspy croak.

"When we crossed out of the border, the smoke shot out of you. It slammed against the wall and we drove out of it." Andy reached up and placed a hand on my shoulder.

I smiled and then shoved the door open. I retched through the open door into the snow bank along the side of the road. When I was done, I pulled the door closed and leaned back against the seat.

"Let's get out of here," I said. "We need to regroup."

I was asleep before the car started moving again.

CHAPTER 14

The aroma of hot pizza brought me back to the world of the living. I sat up, rubbing my greasy hair out of my eyes. My friends were huddled around a small table in the corner of a motel room, devouring the pizza. Evie had a white towel wrapped around her head, ringlets of black hair dripping water on her T-shirt. Andy shoved an entire piece of pizza in his mouth and chewed with gusto as he held the earbuds against his ear. Tristan sat on the couch, a flimsy paper plate held on his lap. He coughed, but the sound was dry and close to normal.

Grant glanced up from his plate and smiled at me. "Hey." He got up and moved over to my bed, sitting down gingerly on the side. He took my hand in his warm one and brought it to his lips, pressing them gently to my palm. The new white T-shirt he wore smelled like the candle my mom used to burn in the kitchen. It was called Cotton Meadow or something.

I shook my head, pulling my hand back and bringing my knees up to my chest. My emotions tumbled through me, with anger and sadness creeping toward the top, dangerously close to spilling over. I blinked back tears and leaned against the headboard. "Where are we?"

"Chillicothe," Andy said around a huge bite. "Hungry?"

My stomach awoke, churning with a growl that rumbled low and long.

He smiled and tossed two pieces on a plate. He brought it over and held it out. "Thanks for, you know, saving me from the smoke monster back there."

I took the plate and nodded, breaking his gaze and staring down at the pizza. A sheen of grease coated the cheese and my stomach roiled again. I passed the plate to Grant. "I need a shower." I stood up and crossed over to the bathroom door, my hand on the knob. I turned back and looked at the room. Our phones were on the dresser, plugged in, but in a tangle of wires. "What time is it?"

"Four," Tristan offered.

"In the morning?"

Evie laughed. It was a nice sound and it pushed the sadness away a bit more. "In the afternoon. Feels like four in the morning, though!"

I let myself into the bathroom, shutting the door and leaning my back against it. I closed my eyes and fought against the tears welling up. Catching a glimpse of myself in the mirror, I squinted. The reflection staring back at me squinted, too, but I couldn't seem to recognize her. I took a few steps forward and rested my hands on the sink, leaning forward until my nose was inches from the glass. The hair hung limply around her face, weighted down by grease and sweat. Her cheeks were drawn in and the lips were chapped, bits of flaky white skin poking up. The girl's eyes were dull and sunken in, deep dark circles framing the bottom lids.

I stared at her for another minute and then shook my head. The girl in the mirror shook her head, too, and then looked away. My hand flew up to my mouth and I stepped back, my hackles raising. Gooseflesh spread along my arms and I took a deep breath. *Turn on the shower. One step.* I took a breath and reached into the tub, turning on the water and letting the warmth spread over my fingers. I peeled off my clothes and left them in the pile of dirty laundry next to the toilet. Averting my eyes from Grant's bloodstained shirt, I swung a towel over the rod and stepped into the water.

As the first droplets hit me, I let out a sigh. The hot water pelted my skin, at once both waking me up and soothing my taut muscles. I tilted my head back into the stream of water. Pinpricks of heat hit my scalp, driving away the grime of the last two days. I looked down at the dirty water spreading around my feet.

A half hour later, I used the towel to wipe the steam from the mirror. This time, I saw myself looking back, cheeks red and eyes sparkling. I smiled at the pile of clean clothes that had been left on the toilet seat. "Thanks, Evie," I called through the door.

"No problem."

I brushed my teeth, pulled on the clothes and yanked a brush through my tangled hair. It fell in a wet sheet onto my shoulders, wrapping me in the leftover warmth of the shower. A cloud of steam bubbled out as I opened the door and stepped into the room.

"Human again?" Andy asked. He sat on the couch next to Tristan, a hand resting lightly on his leg.

I smiled. "More so when I get some food in me."

Grant stood up and handed me the plate. "It's cold."

"It's food." I took the plate and dove into the pizza. I didn't come up for air until I had choked down five slices. Opening the bottle of soda Evie handed me, I drank it in three gulps and let out a burp that shook the lampshades.

"Taking notes, huh?" Andy smiled then patted Tristan on the leg and stood up.

"Um, excuse me," I said. I placed the back of my hand to my mouth.

"Yeah, too late to try for dainty after that belch," he muttered.

"Shut up." I grabbed my phone and swiped at the screen. One email about a sale at the local clothing store and that was it. No missed calls. No texts. I placed it back on the charger.

I felt everyone's eyes on me. "It's fine. It's not like he can text from down there." I felt the lump rise in my throat again and I sat down on the bed.

"Patton had an idea," Andy sat down next to me.

"Um, yeah." She turned in her chair. "You remember when we went Christmas shopping?"

I nodded.

"And remember I went to talk to that history lady about the Weeping Bridge?"

I nodded again.

"Connect the dots, Anderson."

I flipped him off.

Andy bumped me with his shoulder. "She said that lady knew everything about Culvers Grove."

"And you want to go talk to her to figure out how to get down to the basement of the courthouse."

"There she is." He bumped me again. "We thought while we were here…" he let the sentence fade, his eyes never leaving mine.

I caught a sliver of a thought. Something about his little sister. She was playing in the yard when she looked up, fear painted across her features as she looked behind her. The image was gone as quickly. I shook my head.

"Um, yeah. Yeah, that sounds like a plan. When should we go?" I asked.

"The website says the office closes at six," Evie offered.

"So, we'd have to go soon. You feel up to it?" Andy's eyes bore into mine.

I nodded. "Yeah. Are we all going?" I bent my head in Tristan's direction.

"I feel much better," he said. "The pizza helped."

"Being out of that town is helping all of us," Grant said from his spot near the bathroom. He leaned against the doorjamb, his arms folded across his chest.

I felt panic rise up. Even if we found out how to get into the courthouse, my friends would be sick again within minutes.

Andy leaned his head toward me. "Take it one step at a time, Anderson."

I glanced in his direction, my brow knitted.

"Come on," Evie said as she stood up, "let's get going."

We all wrapped up in our coats and gloves and went out to Grant's car. The office was only a few minutes from our motel, so the drive was short, and quiet. No one spoke until we filed out onto the sidewalk. Evie held the door open for us and we darted into the warmth pouring out from the office inside.

"I'll catch up with you guys in a few," Andy said. He shoved his hands in his pockets and started down the sidewalk.

"Where are you going?" I asked. Before the words left my mouth, a flash of a hardware store appeared in my mind. "Oh," I said, and let the door close behind me.

Evie was at the counter, hitting the bell repeatedly as she leaned over to peer around the doorway.

"Can I help you?" A middle-aged woman with bright red hair came around the corner and took the bell from under Evie's hand. She smiled as she placed it a few inches away on the countertop. "Are you all working on a report for school?"

"Um, I don't know if you remember me," Evie started.

The woman smiled again, her plump cheeks squeezing her eyes into cheerful half-moons. "Of course, I remember you. You came in here looking for information on the Weeping Bridge. Did you ever find it?" She cocked an eyebrow over the rim of her pink glasses.

Evie glanced over at me. "You told me that you loved talking to people about Culvers Grove. We were wondering if you had any information about the courthouse."

"Or the cave system under it," Tristan said. He stepped forward and placed his phone on the counter. "This is the only part we've found that has been mapped."

The woman looked down at the phone and then up at Tristan. Her nametag glinted in the fluorescent lighting. It read, Janice, Junior Curator, Historical Society. "You all wouldn't be trying to get into the basement of that old place, would you?"

Tristan smiled. "We've been there. Just trying to get back."

Obviously, it was not the answer she expected. The smile fell from her features and her eyes blazed behind the lenses of her glasses. Energy spilled off of Janice, collecting in pools of excitement around her. She cleared her throat. "You've been in the...basement?"

I nodded. "Yeah. We found a cave on the back of our property and it led to the middle of town and into the basement of the courthouse. That part caved in, though, and we can't get back in."

Janice regarded me for a moment, then leaned her elbows on the counter and rested her chin on her fists. "Cheese and crackers. I mean, I got to visit when I was a kid, but after the accident, they filled it in. What was it like down there?"

Evie shrugged a shoulder. "Dark. Cold." She shuddered.

"What about the well? Was it still there?"

"Yes, it was boarded up, though," I said as Grant's arm slipped around my middle. I welcomed the warmth it provided and leaned into his side. He kissed the top of my head.

"It really wasn't very interesting," Evie said.

Janice swung her gaze over and the corner of her mouth ticked up. "So, why do you all want to go back down there?"

Crap.

Evie looked at me and I blinked.

Tristan rescued the situation. "I know it sounds stupid, but I lost my class ring while I was down there." He shook his head. "I remember I had it on my hand when we went in, and then, on our way out, I realized it wasn't on my finger anymore. My dad just made the first payment on it, and well, he'll kill me if I've lost it." He gave her a winning smile and I held my breath.

Janice stood up straight. "Listen, I've raised three boys who, by the grace of God, lived through all the bad choices they made and grew up to be nice young men. I don't know why you really need to get down there, but it's not my job to help you get hurt." She turned and started tapping away at her keyboard.

Evie looked at me and widened her eyes.

"My dad's going with us," I blurted out.

She looked up at me again. This time she didn't look away. "Your dad?"

"Yeah," I went on. "He went with us the first time. He used to do a lot of rock climbing when he was in college. Before he met my mom. She died. Last year." I clamped my lips down against the onslaught of words beating against the back of my teeth. One of these days, I was really going to have to figure out how to tell a lie.

"I'm sorry, dear," Janice said. She reached a hand out and patted my arm. "That must be hard on you and your father. We lost my husband a few years ago, too. It changes a person." Her eyes went misty for a moment and then she sniffed and recovered. Her gaze was softer this time. "Tell you what. If I could talk to your father, I would feel a lot better about giving you all any more information."

Evie closed her eyes.

"Um, sure." I pulled my phone out of my pocket and scrolled through the numbers. I quickly changed the name on Andy's profile to "Dad" and hit send.

Andy picked up on the first ring. "What's up, Anderson?"

"Hey, Dad." My throat constricted on the word. I swallowed. "We're at the historical society in Chillicothe and the curator wants to speak to you."

"Got it," Andy said.

I handed the phone to Janice.

She looked down at the photo of my dad and then hit speaker. "Hello, Mister…"

"Anderson," Andy provided. "John Anderson."

"Well, Mr. Anderson, my name is Janice -"

Andy cut her off. "Lovely name. My late wife had an Aunt Janice. Wonderful woman. Made amazing apple crisps."

I stifled a giggle.

"I'm calling, sir, because I have your daughter and her friends in the office here and they are looking for information about the cave system under the courthouse. I'm not willing to give them the information without parental consent."

"That's very conscientious of you, Janice. Safe, too. My partner recently tried a case - Monroe versus Smith - where a man was convicted of involuntary manslaughter for the death of a girl he served alcohol to at his son's party. Terrible case. Can't be too careful these days. Society as a whole grows more litigious with each passing day, don't you agree?"

Janice cleared her throat. "I'm sorry, Mr. Anderson - "

"Call me John."

"Um, yes, John. I'm sorry."

I tilted my head. The color had risen in Janice's cheeks as she talked and her eyes were doing that half-moon thing again.

Evie leaned in. "It's maroon all around her. She likes him." She paused. "Which is wrong on so, so many levels."

I tucked my chin into my coat.

"Your daughter told me that you would be going into the caves with them?"

"Oh, of course. I wouldn't dream of letting them go in by themselves. I had years of training in cave diving in South America back in my younger days. Have you ever traveled there?"

"Um, no. I don't get away from my job much. Um," she laughed nervously, "do I have your permission to release information to your daughter?"

"Sure, sure. We're planning an expedition for next weekend. You should come with us if you're not too busy."

I mentally kicked Andy in the shins.

"Well, I don't know. I haven't been to Culvers Grove in a while, though. It might be nice. Listen, I'll write my number on the map and you call me if you feel like it sometime."

"Absolutely. Nice chatting with you, Janice."

"You, too." She handed the phone back to me.

I put it to my ear.

"How'd I do?"

"Perfect," I said. "We'll be home soon. Love you."

"Love you, too, cupcake."

I hit the button on my phone and shoved it in my pocket.

Janice walked around the end of the counter. "Come on," she said, beckoning us, "I have what you all are looking for in the back room."

CHAPTER 15

Janice led us into the back room of the office. She skirted around file cabinets and shelving filled with boxes.

"Sorry about the mess," she said over her shoulder. "We're attempting to go all digital, but it's only another curator and me, and she's only part-time. I have most of the marriage records entered for the city and surrounding counties. It's a big job."

"Culvers Grove isn't in your county, though," I said as I stepped around a pile of boxes on the worn green carpet.

She stopped. "Culvers Grove is a…well, it's sort of a pet project of mine. I got interested in its history when the hauntings started."

I raised my eyebrows. "The hauntings?"

She looked down and shook her head. "I know it sounds crazy, but it seems like there are more ghost stories than there should be for a town that small. My late husband said I watched too many paranormal shows on cable, but I really think there's something going on there."

I glanced over at Evie. Her eyes bore into me.

"Stories like the Weeping Bridge?" I asked.

"That was the first one, but there are so many others, dating all the way back to the eighteen hundreds."

"What other ghost stories?" I asked. The room was suddenly too hot and I shrugged out of my coat.

Janice grabbed a box from a top shelf and placed it on a card table. She opened the top and started pulling out papers. "There was a story about a woman killed there before it was even really a town. Legend has it, she was in love with a member of the Sac and Fox tribe and her parents didn't approve. She snuck out one day to meet him and was killed."

"What happened?" Tristan sat down in one of the folding chairs. He leafed through the papers she placed next to the box.

"Well, no one knows for sure. When she didn't come home, the father gathered some of the other men from surrounding homesteads and they ambushed the tribe's settlement. Ah, here it is." Janice pulled a weathered leather-bound book from the box. "This is his journal. Here, I marked the place."

I took the book from her hands and gently opened it to the page indicated by a small slip of paper sticking up from it. The pages were yellow and brittle and the writing was virtually unreadable. I leaned down to let the light catch the page and started reading. "Twenty-seventh day of October, the year of our Lord eighteen twelve. Upon reaching the settlement of the savages, Brother Johnathon rode ahead, seeking out the man who killed my dearest Faith. The men of the village were gone when we arrived. Held the women and children near the edge. I was bid come hither by my friend. In a small structure in the back, a man stood, swaying back and forth seemingly greatly vexed. White hair hung over his face, hiding it from my view. I shouted again and when I did, the savage looked upon me with hollow eyes. Dear Lord, his eyes were hollow."

The entry stopped there. I looked up. "What happened?"

"The village was then burned to the ground, along with all of the women and children in it. Thirteen victims. The Sac and Fox tribe relocated after that, claiming the ground was full of a bad spirit. It's said the young girl's ghost walks along the meadows of the town under light of the full moon, looking for her lover."

I shivered. The image of that morning's vision slammed into my brain. The Native Americans greeting their families. The children running around. Had this been the settlement that had been burned by the settlers?

"Whoa," Evie breathed, shaking me from my thoughts. She picked up a photograph and handed it to me. "This looks just like you, St. Louis."

I took the photo and stared. "It's my great grandmother. Um, Sarah." The vision of her being pulled into the portal by Sam tore at my heart and I blinked my eyes. In the photo, she sat with her back ramrod straight in a chair next to my great grandfather. Her dress was white and flowing and he was in a dark suit, his mustache overtaking his mouth.

"James and Sarah Miller," Janice read from the back of the photo. "This is your family?"

I swallowed and nodded.

She looked at me for a minute more and then dove back into the box. When she came up, she held an old newspaper in her hand. "Samuel Johnson killed in an accident."

I nodded. "He was killed during construction of the courthouse in 1904. He was only nineteen."

"You grew up in Culvers Grove?"

I shook my head. "No, my dad did, though. We moved here a few months ago."

Janice regarded me for another minute. "I knew your grandmother, um, Lydia, right?"

I nodded. "Yeah. We're living in her old house."

"The map?" Tristan asked.

"Oh, yes." Janice disappeared among the shelves again.

"You think that was the Native American you saw in the grove of trees this morning?" Evie asked.

I shook my head. "I don't know."

"Do you remember the first time we went into the cave on your farm? You saw them there, too. Were they the same ones?"

I rubbed at my eyes. "I don't think so. I was really freaked out, though, so I don't remember much about what I saw."

"You drew a picture of it," Tristan said.

"I'd forgotten about that. It's in the book at my house, though."

"No, it's not," Evie said. "You grabbed the book when we packed. It's in the bag with our clothes. Hey, where's Andy?"

I shook my head again.

"I'll go check on him." Evie yawned. "I need the cold air."

She wandered out and Grant sat down next to Tristan.

"Do you think she has a map?" he asked.

"I hope so." The warmth was lulling me into a state of comfort. My muscles ached and my eyelids were heavy. I yawned, too, and sat down heavily in a chair. "This has been the longest day ever."

"Never. Ending."

Something nagged at the back of my mind. I tried to follow the elusive thought as it twisted away from me down the chasms of my tired mind.

"Here's what I was looking for." Janice came out, holding a roll of paper up like a torch. "This is the only map I know of that shows the Howling Cavern."

A shiver ran through me and I was instantly awake. "The Howling Cavern?"

She smiled and swept everything from the table back into the box carefully. "It's not as scary as it sounds." She spread the paper out on the table. Black pen squiggles covered the surface.

"Um, what am I looking at?" I asked.

Tristan stood up and pored over the paper. "It's the entire cave system!" His voice held reverence. "The whole thing!"

"It's the only copy I know of," Janice said. "Now, if I'm correct, your farm is located here?" She pointed to the paper with a fingernail that had chipped red polish.

I squinted and tried to get the lay of the land. "I'm not sure."

"The highway runs right along here," she said, tracing a path.

"Oh, yeah. That looks familiar."

"There's the quarry," Tristan pointed.

"And the courthouse must be here," Grant said.

Janice moved his finger an inch to the left. "Right there."

Tristan gauged the distance between the two. "That's almost seven miles, as the crow flies."

"Longer with all the twists and turns." Grant sounded defeated.

My heart dropped as I stared at the spot under his finger. My dad was there. I had to get to him. I didn't care if I had to walk for twenty miles, I would get to him. I felt a twinge in my head and shook it, then looked up. "Sorry?"

Grant peered at me. "I asked if you were okay."

"Yeah. I'm fine." I blinked.

"I don't see any other entrances," Tristan breathed.

"There are only a few that are accessible. This one here," she pointed at a place near a lake, "is covered by water, and this one has been closed since a cave-in in the early eighties."

"Looks like the quarry's it," Tristan mumbled.

"My suggestion would be to enter here," Janice said, "through the Howling Cavern. Back in the 1920s, during Prohibition, the locals opened up a speakeasy underground there. The cavern was enormous and they had bands play there and everything!" Her voice amped up a notch. "They called it the Howling Cavern after Toots McGee played a gig. People said that his horn made the entire place howl."

"How did they keep it from the police?"

Janice smiled. "Who do you think were the biggest customers? My granddad said he went there once, just to see what all the fuss was about, and he saw Sheriff Jenkins bellied up to the bar, foot tapping along to the music. In uniform and everything!" She laughed.

Tristan stared at the map. "That gets us almost to the center of town. Are you sure the entrance is still accessible?"

Janice nodded. "You remember those boys that I wasn't sure were going to make it to adulthood? The oldest two dared the youngest to spend a night there. They ended up scaring him so badly that he slept on the couch for a month, but I know it was open then. That would be, say, about six years ago now."

Tristan looked up at me. "Should we go get your dad?"

I nodded and stood up. "I need to go outside for a minute." I raised my voice. "It was nice to meet you and thank you so much for the information."

Janice smiled. "Of course. I'll go make a copy of the map and those photos, too, if you'd like."

Tristan and Grant offered to wait while I went outside. The second I hit the cold air, I was wide awake, my senses heightened. The thought that had been dancing around the periphery of my consciousness appeared in front of me as if saying, "What took you so long?"

I shook my head and turned to go back into the building, opening the photos on my phone. I scrolled through several until I found what I was looking for.

"Janice?"

She looked up from the copier.

I held the phone up. "These were on the wall of the cave on the back of our property. Evie and I found them when we went exploring one night. I took a picture because I didn't know what they meant."

Janice came to the counter and took my phone from me. She stared down at the picture I'd taken of the carvings in the wall of the cave.

"Do you know what they mean?" I asked.

She shook her head then looked over the rims of her glasses at me. "If you send this to me, I'll do some research on it. See what I can find?"

I nodded and punched her number into my phone. I sent it off with a whoosh sound from my phone and brought up the text that appeared from Evie.

Get out here. Now.

"Thanks," I said over my shoulder as I hurried out the door again. I stood on the sidewalk, looking around. I finally saw them standing across the street on top of a huge hill, their footprints in the snow winding a trail up to their silhouettes.

I made my way up the hill, panting as I climbed through the snow.

"What...is...so...important?" I stood doubled over, catching my breath at the top.

"Look," Evie pointed in the distance.

I squinted, staring across the miles of dark country dotted by lights every once in a while. "I don't see anything."

Evie turned to look at me. "It's Culvers Grove. I can see it all, St. Louis. I can see the disturbance. It's - it's like a huge...*blister*." Her eyes filled with tears.

Andy put his arm around my shoulder as I stared out into the distance again, toward the town, toward my dad, toward my family.

CHAPTER 16

Grant and I sat at the table, the lamp casting an orange glow on our hands interlocked on the table's surface. Grant's hands were strong, but gentle at the same time. I sat mesmerized as I watched his thumb rub the back of my hand in a comforting motion. The others sat on one of the beds, the map spread out between them. Andy had an earbud shoved in his right ear. He insisted he listen to the spirit box recording from the night before. I didn't think he'd learn anything more than I had from the conversation with my grandma, but more power to him. Maybe he'd hear something I hadn't.

"You're tired," Grant said, his voice gruff. He cleared his throat.

"So are you," I countered. He was right, though. The exhaustion pulsed through me with an almost palpable sensation. I had to stay awake, though. "Listen, I'm sorry about earlier. About the gas station. What I said about, well about everything."

He squeezed my hand. "Marissa, I know you didn't mean it. You were scared and worried about me. I would've done the same thing in your position."

"No," I shook my head and pulled my hand away, "you wouldn't have. You would have handled everything without pushing me away."

"I would have if I thought it would keep you safe. Marissa, if I could do this for you," he drew his hand into a fist. "If I could keep you from getting hurt..." The sentence hung in the space between us.

I placed my hand over his. "I know." I wanted to say other things, to thank him for being there, for coming to our rescue, for believing in me. The words spun in my head, though, and I couldn't untangle them to make them make sense. Instead, I squeezed his hand. "I love you."

"I love you, too."

"I hate to break up this incredibly romantic moment, but you need to hear this." Andy held out the earbud to me.

I let go of Grant's hand and took the bud, placing it in my ear. I nodded at Andy and he hit the button.

Nothing but static.

I looked up at Andy.

"Give it a second. You have to listen close to hear it."

I cupped my hands around my ears, blocking out the noise of the room. More static, then a voice came through. It was my grandma.

"...know how...stop it...I'll be safe...tell Marissa I love...have to get the lock..."

The recording stopped there. I stared up at Andy. "What's she talking about?"

He shrugged. "She has to get the lock?"

I shook my head. "I don't know. I don't know where she went. Do you think she went back to the house?"

He sat down on the edge of the bed, passing the recorder to Evie. She listened, her head bowed over her crossed legs.

"I don't think so. She knows that Sam is looking for her. I don't think she'd go back to the place he last saw her." Andy rubbed his chin, the raspy sound of the stubble carrying in the silent room.

"I don't know then." My head was swimming and I felt the drag of exhaustion pulling me down. A thought again. It fluttered, gently nudging my memory. "Wait! She told me that she had a baby that died. Do you think she went to be there? She said she always went there to think."

"Do you know where it is?" Grant asked.

"Up until last night, I didn't even know about the baby," I said. I rubbed my hands over my eyes. "I don't even know who would know anymore."

"We all need some sleep." Andy gently took the phone from Tristan's grasp. "Especially you. Get some sleep, please?" He reached out and placed his hand on Tristan's cheek.

Tristan closed his eyes and leaned into Andy's palm. He nodded. "You're right. Sleep is what we need." Getting up, he folded the papers from the bed and placed them on the table.

After a flurry of activity and sleeping arrangements discussed, we all bunked down and turned out the lights. I set the silent alarm on my phone for midnight and let my eyes close. My breathing settled into the same rhythm as Grant's as he lay behind me, his arm draped over my side. I didn't even have time to say "goodnight" before I drifted off.

***

My phone buzzed next to me. I swiped my finger across the screen and lay in the darkness for a moment, listening to my friends breathing around me. A lump on the other bed shifted and I heard one of them begin snoring. Smiling, I peeked over the sleeping form of

Grant at the couch. Evie lay with one arm over her head and one leg poking out from under the blanket. Her face was almost completely covered by her hair and she breathed open-mouthed.

As slowly as I could, I slipped out from under the covers and leaned down to grab my boots from the floor. I shoved my phone in my jeans pocket and pulled my hair into a tail. My coat was next to the door and I made my way across the floor on tiptoes. With my coat slung over my arm, I reached out for the doorknob, barely breathing as I turned the lock and then the knob. The door opened silently and the outside noises were muffled by the blanket of snow still on the ground. I stood in the doorway, the green light from the sign in the parking lot spilling across the carpet. Biting my bottom lip, I pulled the door closed behind me. It closed with a quiet click and I stood frozen, making sure the noise hadn't woken anyone inside.

The air was frigid. Shrugging on my coat, I shoved my feet into my boots then bent down to tie each one. I stood up, my breath hanging in a cloud around my head as I stared out into the quiet night. If I could make it to the highway, I could catch a ride with someone back to Culvers Grove. I hesitated. I didn't know the exact statistics for girls who got into strange cars getting murdered, but I didn't think the odds were good. Scratch that. Maybe I'd head over to the diner across the road and call a cab. They had cabs in this part of the state, right? My head swam and I shook it to clear it.

"Fine, Marissa," I whispered, "but you have to get there somehow."

I took a step past the front of Grant's car and headed toward the highway. A noise caught my attention and I almost wet myself when a dark figure came out from behind the car. My breath caught in my throat and I backpedaled, my hands flying up in front of my face.

"You're going to have to teach me that move, Anderson." Andy stepped into the light, his face quizzical. "Whatcha' doin'?"

I stared at him. "I-I could ask you the same thing."

He spun a tool in his hand. "Yeah, but I actually have an excuse for being out here at midnight. You," he pointed the tool at me, "don't."

I backed up and rested against the building. "I don't want anyone else to get hurt." Tears burned my eyes. "I can't let you get hurt."

Andy stood across from me, his arms folded across his chest. "You're a piece of work, you know that?"

"Excuse me?"

"You know, I am so sick of this being all about you, Marissa."

I started to object but he went on.

"Everything is about you. *You* being able to see ghosts. *You* wanting to help everyone. *Your* family. You,

you, *you*." He jabbed the tool at me with each iteration. "It's been the Marissa Anderson show now for months and I, for one, have had it!"

Anger burned my insides, spilling over into my limbs. I shook with rage. "Are you kidding me right now?" I hissed. "Are you actually telling me that you think I've done any of this on purpose, for, for, *attention*?"

He shook his head, and then peered up at me. "I don't think that at all. I think you're scared and you're tired, and you think you're the only one who can stop this thing."

"Um, turns out, I *am* the only thing that can stop it. I'm what it wants."

"So, what was your plan tonight anyway? Hitchhike to Culvers Grove? March into the quarry? Get down to the basement and demand that whatever's down there hand over your dad?" His eyes blazed. "Is that it?"

A tear rolled down my cheek. "Stop it," I whispered.

"No! I'm not going to stop until you get it through your head that you are not alone in this! This is bigger than you, Anderson! Heck, this is bigger than all of us put together. This is *our* town, *our* families, *our* friends. How dare you be so selfish!"

"Stop," I whispered again, wrapping my arms around my middle. "Please."

He stepped forward, his face a foot from mine. "Marissa, what about my sister? My parents? What do you think is going to happen when they die? Where will their spirits go? What about my soul?"

I looked up. His eyes were filled with tears. I blinked, my chin quivering.

"We're all from that town, St. Louis."

I turned to see Evie standing in the doorway. Grant and Tristan stood behind her, faces lit up in the green glow.

Andy reached out and placed his hand on my shoulder. "It started out as your fight, but now it's all of ours. We're in this together." His eyes searched mine. "Do you get that?"

I nodded, the tears spilling out.

"Do you really? You really get it this time, right? We're not just your friends, Anderson."

"We're your family," Evie said.

I nodded again. "I get it," I managed to squeak out. "I do."

Andy gathered me in a hug and I pulled him to me.

"I'm sorry," I said against his coat.

"Come on. Let's go inside before we freeze." He turned me toward the door and I walked in. Everyone gathered me in a hug and I let the tears flow.

CHAPTER 17

Back inside the motel bathroom, I pulled myself together. Splashing water on my face helped calm the red splotches that sprang up on my cheeks from a combination of the cold and my tears. My chest still rose and fell with emotion. *They're right, you know.* I nodded at my reflection. *I know.* She stared at me, her eyes never wavering. I dropped my gaze. *I can't do it alone.*

But, they might get hurt.

I swung my gaze up to the mirror again. My brow furrowed, forming two vertical lines between my eyebrows. I flipped the light off and opened the door quietly but was greeted by everyone sitting up with the lights on in the room.

"Listen, guys…" I stood shifting from foot to foot in front of the bathroom door.

"All's forgiven, Anderson. Just promise us that you're not a flight risk anymore?"

I smiled and sat down on the bed next to Evie. "Promise."

"Look at this." Tristan had the map of the cave system spread out on the table. A lone lamp cast its glow onto the paper. "Right here is Marissa's house." He pointed with a pen to a red X then swung the pen in an arc to the east. "Here's the Weeping Bridge." The pen dragged in another arc. "The lake, Hannah's house, the quarry, the place where Beth was killed in the car accident, and the road where we tried to get out the first time. Those are all the places we've seen Sam and the ghosts."

I stood up and stared over his shoulder. "It makes a circle."

Tristan looked up at me. "Right. Around the whole town. And, guess what's in the middle."

"The courthouse," Evie breathed from beside me.

A shiver rolled through me. "That's how they're moving around."

Everyone looked at me.

I swallowed. "It's sending them through the caves."

Everyone continued to stare at me.

I threw up my hands. "Ghosts have to stay near where they died. They're, um, tied to the place, right, and they can only move away from that spot a couple of different ways."

"They either go through a portal," Grant offered.

"Or they take over a doll." Evie shuddered.

"Or, they're part of my bloodline." I stepped back and rubbed my arm. "Grandma said she had always been able to travel around freely, but she stayed because of my grandpa. She was happy."

"But, she couldn't leave the town."

"Grant and I were talking about that on the way out of town the first night. He thinks the fact that my ancestors can move around freely made the…" I trailed off, searching for a word to describe what I'd seen under the courthouse.

"The darkness?" Andy offered.

I nodded. "Yeah, the darkness wanted to use them to get out. That's why it took Sam and then Sarah."

"Wait a minute," Evie whispered to me. "Sam told me he couldn't leave the courthouse. If he was like, well, like *you,* then why was he stuck there?"

She had me there. I rolled it around in my mind.

"When they couldn't help it get out, it set its sights on Marissa," Grant said.

"Because she has one foot in this world and one in the other," Andy said. "She's, um, well, she's alive."

I nodded again. Sitting down on the edge of the bed, I put my head in my hands. "That's why it wants me. It thinks I can help it get out."

"Your dad is like you, though. Doesn't it already have what it needs to get out?"

I shook my head. "My dad has the same abilities, but he's worked for years to push it away. He can't see the same things I can. I don't think it can use him like it could me. I think my dad is a means to get to me."

"Why is it gathering all the other spirits, then?" Tristan leaned over the map, peering at it as if the answer would present itself if he stared hard enough.

"It makes it more powerful. It's getting stronger," Grant said.

"That's why it's able to affect the living, now."

I shook my head. "But what does it have to gain from that?"

Andy smiled. "A ghost *army*, Anderson? Who wouldn't want that?"

"I wish I knew what it was and why it wanted to get out," I said. I laid back on the bed and rubbed my temples.

"I'm assuming you're looking for more than world domination, here?" Andy patted my leg.

"If it's a demon, then that's your answer," Tristan said. "I think it's been there forever and it's been gathering power so that it can get out of wherever it's trapped."

His words were met with silence as we all mulled them over. The overhead light burned into my retinas and I closed my eyes.

"How are we going to stop it?" I asked, my voice scratchy in my throat.

No one said anything.

"Yeah, that's what I was afraid of." A small ball of light danced along the backs of my eyelids, the aftereffect of the bright globe hanging from the popcorn ceiling stained brown by years of cigarette smoke. The ball of light danced, growing until it took over my entire field of vision. I squeezed my eyes shut, focusing on the brightness. A figure took shape and wavered in front of me. It was the man I saw in the grove of trees.

He reached out to me. "Ugísa^n."

His face turned into the spirit I saw beneath the courthouse. Bathed in light, his countenance was kind and welcoming, but strained. He looked like he had the weight of the world on his shoulders.

Maybe he does.

I sat straight up. "It's him!"

The group watched me while I dove across the room to the bag on the floor. I yanked the book from the bottom and sat on the carpet, cross-legged as I thumbed through the book.

"He's in the drawing, too," Andy whispered.

I threw him a glance and then found the pictures I'd drawn wedged between the pages that told the story of the Weeping Bridge. A moment flashed by of Evie and me sitting on the floor of the Purple Unicorn looking through it for the first time. I shook my head and grabbed the papers, spreading them out around me on the floor. Sadness crept into my heart as I relived all the places we had visited and all the spirits we had been so eager to help. When I saw the picture I was looking for, I grabbed it and pulled it up so it was practically touching my nose. I looked at the pencil sketches, poring over the faces of the men moving around the fire in the cave. No one near the fire looked like the man I had seen in the grove, though. I scanned the picture again, certain I had missed something.

Look closer. He's there.

I glanced up at Andy again. He nodded and I bent down over the picture again.

"Here," Tristan said, moving the lamp from its spot by the television to the floor near me.

"Thanks," I mumbled. I scanned over the faces again. None of them looked familiar. Then, something in the background pulled my attention. There, behind the group at the fire, was a man crouched down near a gaping hole in the wall of the cavern. He had his hand up, tears streaming down his face as he carved something into the wall with a crude chisel and rock. I didn't recognize him, but as I looked closer, I could see a ghostly face in the darkness of the hole.

It was the man.

"It's him." I pointed and looked up at my friends.

They were gathered in a half circle around me.

"More words would be good here, Anderson."

"The man I saw in the grove of trees this morning, he was the same one I saw underneath the courthouse. He was bathed in light and I didn't get a good look at him, but I know it's the same person."

"Was that the old spirit Sam went to talk to when I was in a coma?"

"I think so. I think he planned to talk to that man, but the darkness tricked him into talking to it instead."

"And it convinced him to bring me to the courthouse so it could get to you."

I nodded.

"Maybe because he was tied to the light."

I looked up at Grant. "Tied to the light?"

"What Evie asked you earlier. Why couldn't Sam leave the courthouse before? You told us that you thought he was doing good things when you saw him take Thomas. What if when he died, his spirit went into the light instead of the dark?"

"He was helping the man in the light help ghosts stay happy so that the darkness couldn't get to them." I closed my eyes for a moment. "The darkness only takes spirits that are in turmoil. It can't get to them if they're happy."

Grant nodded. "It makes sense. He's being used by the darkness now, right? Well, as an instrument of the darkness, his reach is only as far as the darkness can reach."

Andy's eyes sparked. "He has to use the same tunnels the darkness uses because he's part of the darkness. That makes sense!" He scooted up to the edge of the bed and pointed at the map. "All the places we've seen him have been connected by the cave system. The entrance on your farm." He knit his brow. "You said that you saw him rise out of the water where Thomas died. There's an entrance, but it's probably underwater."

"But that was a vision from the past."

"If he was being used by the light to help ghosts, he was an instrument of the light."

"So," something coalesced in my mind, "he had to use the cave system to get around then. That's why he was trapped there." I put my hand over my mouth.

"What's wrong?" Evie asked.

I looked up at her. "Do you think he knew he'd be trapped there when he agreed to help the light?"

Realization spread over her features. She sat down heavily on the other bed. "If so, then he knew he was choosing not to see his family again. He *knew* he wasn't going to be able to see his baby girl grow up." Her voice was filled with emotion. "That sucks."

I nodded. "Yeah, everything about this sucks."

My phone buzzed and I grabbed it off the nightstand. "It's Janice." I opened the text and read it out loud. "She says the carving is written in the Ioway, Otoe-Missouria language. It says 'É^e Náwu Pí arámañisge hdaho, hagún da ke.'"

"What's it mean?"

I scrolled down. "It's a traditional Ioway blessing for those left behind."

I typed a message and hit send. The answer was almost immediate.

"Check this out," I said. "Ugísa^n means 'help.'"

CHAPTER 18

"Are you asleep?" Grant's breath was a whisper on my ear.

I shook my head and turned over, tucking into the warm space under the covers. He wrapped me in his arms and squeezed.

"Don't worry about your dad." His finger stroked the side of my face.

I closed my eyes and sighed. "That's like telling me not to breathe."

He chuckled. "He's going to be fine. We all are. I have a good feeling about this."

I opened my eyes and looked up at him. His features were hidden in the darkness of the room. "I wish I had your optimism."

His hand faltered. "It's not optimism. It's the way I feel. You know, ever since I met you, everything has gone right in my life."

I narrowed my eyes.

He chuckled again. "Quit giving me that look."

"You can't even see me."

"I know you're giving me the look, though."

"Shut up."

"Think about it. Before I met you, I was biding my time, going to school and working odd jobs. It's like I was..." He trailed off, his hand falling to the blanket on my side.

"What?"

"Well, it's like I was waiting for you."

I shifted, knocking his hand from my side as I moved away from him.

"Don't do that."

"Don't do what?"

"That. Every time I bring up something about us, you pull away."

I paused. "I don't mean to."

"Why are you so afraid of letting me get close to you?"

I stared at the darkness. "Are you seriously asking me that? Have you met me?"

He chuckled again, but this time, it held a note of sadness. "I know you've lost a lot of people."

"Try everyone I've ever cared about."

"I'm still around."

"Give it a couple days."

The rhythmic breathing from the other bed and couch marked the minutes passing between us. I opened my mouth a couple of times to talk, but I couldn't say what I really wanted to say. *I love you and I'm scared. I'm scared that loving you means that you'll go away.*

Finally, Grant pulled me close, his hands intertwining in my hair as he kissed me. I let him hold me then, reveling in the safety his arms provided. For the next few hours, I could pretend that everything was back to normal. That Grant and I were worried about nothing more serious than what we were going to do that weekend. My eyes closed and I breathed deeply the lingering scent of his cologne.

"…love you, Marissa…" he breathed.

"I love you, too," I murmured against his chest.

✳✳✳

"It's safe. They have all their clothes on."

My eyes flew open and then slammed down again against the onslaught of the bright sun's rays pouring through the broken slats of the blinds. I squinted one eye open.

Evie stood next to the bed, her arms folded and her head cocked to the side. "Time to get up, lover boy." She pulled the covers from Grant's sleeping form. "Time to let me check those cuts on your stomach." She held up a white plastic bag. "Hope you don't mind that I used your debit card, St. Louis."

"Um," I sat up, "what for?"

She smiled and dumped the contents on the wrinkled bedspread. "Adhesive for Grant's cuts, caffeine pills for you and me, anti-nausea medicine for Andy," she paused to toss the box to him, "and cold medicine for Tristan." The bottle flew across the room and right through Tristan's outstretched hands. He leaned over and retrieved it from the floor.

Evie stood smiling. "I thought it would help."

"Good thinking, Patton," Andy said, throwing off the covers and pushing his feet into his shoes.

"Yeah," Grant said, "that stuff should gain us some time in there."

I stood up, my legs strong and my head clear. The sleep really had done me good. I scanned the room, my stomach flip-flopping. "You know," I started.

Andy stood up and clapped a hand on my shoulder. "You do understand if you say that we don't have to come with you, I'll have to deck you, right?"

I smiled.

"Good. I was hoping our talk last night settled it. We're all going in today and we're going to get your dad and save the town from the BB."

I looked around at the others. Evie shrugged.

"Um, the BB?"

"Yeah, the Big Baddie."

"Oh, I see. Makes perfect sense." I rolled my eyes.

"Didn't you ever watch scary movies as a kid?"

I shook my head. "I don't even watch them now."

"Well, the one thing I learned is that, once the thing scaring everyone has a name, it's a little less scary. When it's an abstract, it's more terrifying."

Tristan smoothed the comforter down over his pillow and went around making Andy's side of the bed. "That was awfully deep for this early in the morning."

Andy let a burp rip forth that echoed in the small room. He looked around, scratching his belly. "Yep, that's about it for the day. I have to pee." He disappeared into the bathroom.

"Charming," Tristan mumbled, moving to the couch and beginning to fold the blanket Evie slept under. He saw me watching and smiled sheepishly. "I know they have people to do this, but it makes me feel better to have something to do."

I smiled back. It felt forced, though, and I turned my attention to Evie and Grant. They had settled on the chairs in the corner and she had the lamp focused on his stomach. I leaned over, trying to get a better look at the scratches.

"They look a *lot* better," Evie said. "The skin's hardly broken anymore. See?" She moved out of my way.

The scratches did look better. The skin around was welted, but much less red and angry than it had been the day before. I watched as Evie spread the adhesive along the scratches, effectively gluing them shut. When she was done, she placed new white gauze over them and taped the gauze down.

My own stomach fluttered as I watched her fingers press the tape into the hills and valleys of the cut muscles. I imagined my fingers tracing down the center of his six pack and I felt a flush rise to my cheeks. *Good grief, Marissa.* I shook my head.

Grant watched me, his mouth drawn up on one side in a half grin.

"What?" I asked defensively, busying myself with packing up our stuff in the duffel bag.

"Nothing. Nothing at all." His voice held a hint of laughter in it and I felt my cheeks flush again.

"Anyone else want to shower before we go?" Andy asked as he emerged from the bathroom, his hair wet and water dripping from his chin.

We all took turns using the bathroom and called the diner next door to get breakfast delivered. When I was done with my shower, I came out to a room filled with the delicious smells of breakfast. The scent of bacon made my stomach growl and tears rush to my eyes. It smelled like my grandparents. *My grandma.* I froze, the wheels turning in my head.

"She knows what it is."

Everyone turned to look at me. Andy had half a strip of bacon hanging from his mouth.

"What's up, St. Louis?"

I started walking, three steps this way, then turned. "When I went to wake her up, she said that there were things in this town that I shouldn't mess with. And, then, when I woke Sarah up, she said something like, 'then, it's started.'"

"They know what the BB is?" Tristan asked.

I stopped walking for a moment. I guess the term was going to catch on. I shook my head and started walking again. "I don't know if they know what it is, but they didn't seem surprised that people, *ghosts*, were being taken."

"St. Louis?"

I stopped and looked up.

"How does that help us?"

I drew my eyebrows together. "Um, I don't know, but I think it's interesting that they both seemed to know something about what was going on."

"Come get something to eat. We have to talk to you." Grant's voice was gentle. *Too gentle.*

I squinted at them. "What's going on?"

"We, um," Evie looked at Andy.

He shoved an entire biscuit in his mouth and talked around it. "We think we can get you down to your dad, but not before the BB sniffs you out. We need a distraction." His eyes came up to meet mine. "Your grandma."

I took a step back. "No."

"Do you have any other ideas?" Evie asked.

"If we go in, we won't make it very far with you," Andy said.

Grant cleared his throat. "You're like a beacon. Your whole family, really."

Andy finished eating and licked his fingers. "And people who have a part of you in them."

I squinted again.

He regarded me. "Really? You can't feel it? How do you think I knew to be outside last night to stop you?"

I thought about the glimpse of his little sister playing in the yard. "You feel it, too?"

He nodded. "I think when you pulled the smoke out of me, a little of us, um, intertwined." He leaned over to Grant. "Don't worry. I'm still totally into dudes."

Grant smiled. "Got it."

Evie spoke up. "When I passed through your body, I felt connected to you for a long time. It's not as strong now, but I used to be able to tell how you were feeling all the time."

"Because you could see the colors."

She shook her head. "I didn't realize it at the time, but it was more than seeing the colors. With most people, I saw the colors. With you, I *felt* them."

"And now, I've put a target on your backs." I shook my head.

"A target that may prove *very* useful." Andy cocked his eyebrow.

"But we're no match for your spirit," Evie offered.

"We need someone to lure the BB's hench-ghosts to the other side of the town while you're going in through the old speakeasy." Andy stopped eating to look up at me. His eyes caught mine. *You know it's the only way, Anderson.*

I shook my head. *Stop doing that.*

Too late now. I'm in your head. ooooOOOOoo!

I narrowed my eyes at him.

Andy laughed and held his hands up. "Okay, okay. No more. I promise."

I sighed, and then looked up at him again. *You're sure it's the only way?*

He nodded solemnly.

"I don't know where to find her," I said.

Really? No idea?

I sat down and stared at the Styrofoam container of eggs. Suddenly, the thought that had escaped me last night slammed into my conscious brain and I nodded. I knew exactly who would know where my grandma was. *Melanie.*

Nice going, Anderson.

Thanks.

I cleared my throat. "I'm going to eat breakfast and then we're going to go find my grandma."

CHAPTER 19

We stood outside the motel room, the plan fresh in our minds, staring at Grant's car. The sleek powder blue was broken up by splashes of dirty snow and there was a long scratch running along the passenger door.

"I'll get that buffed out," Andy said, readjusting the strap of the bag on his shoulder.

The scratch wasn't what we were staring at, though.

Perched on the passenger door was a bright green side mirror with tinges of rust running along the back. It was shaped like the head of a rocket and looked completely and totally out of place on Grant's car.

"What is *that*?" Grant nodded his head toward the abomination.

"That," Andy walked over to stand next to the car, "is an example of the vehicular hay day of this great nation."

Grant popped the trunk.

"You see, the auto parts store here in the teeming metropolis of Chillicothe was running short on their supply of side mirrors for a 1968 Chevelle."

"Huh," I muttered.

Evie turned to me and raised her eyebrow.

"I thought it was a Mustang."

Andy and Grant gaped at me.

"Get over it." I rolled my eyes. "So, I don't know cars."

Andy stared at me for a moment longer and then swung the bag into the trunk with a grunt. "Since they were in short supply of the mirror needed, I instead purchased this fine piece of American engineering with which to replace your missing mirror."

Grant got in and turned the engine over. "Missing because of *you*," he said, glancing in the rearview at Andy as the rest of the group got in.

I climbed in next to him and pulled the door shut gingerly. Grant tossed me a wink and waggled his eyebrows.

He's not really mad, you know.

I know. Andy reached up and squeezed my shoulder. "Anyway, it fits perfectly and I think, *I* think," he stressed, "it gives your car some much needed character."

Grant glanced up in the rearview again as he pulled out onto the highway. A whole night of snow plowing combined with the warmer temperatures and sun this morning had done wonders for the road and we were soon flying down the highway.

"Fine. It's from a 1982 Pinto," Andy said.

I stifled a giggle.

"But the guy who owned the car last was really cool, man. He was a door-to-door salesman. Vacuum cleaners. On the weekends, he volunteered as a coach for little league games and spent his mornings helping at the soup kitchens."

I turned around to look at Andy.

"Kansas City. Power and Light district," he said by way of explanation.

I raised an eyebrow.

"His name was Walter Panucik and his family were immigrants from the Czech Republic. He loved kids and always wanted some, but Harriet couldn't have children. Kind of a sad story if you think about it."

"Did they give you all that information at the auto parts store?" Grant asked.

I stared at Andy. Something was solidifying in my head. "He didn't hear the story at the store. Hold on," I reached into my pocket and fished around for my mother's ring. I pulled it out and held it in the sun. It glinted and I swallowed the lump in my throat. "Here. Hold this." I passed him the ring.

Andy took the ring and peered at it. His brow furrowed. Then, he looked up at me, a wide smile breaking on his face. "This was your mother's. Oh, man, the day your dad gave her this was, like, the happiest one of her life. He was a lot less gray back then, wasn't he?"

I nodded, tears springing to my eyes.

"It was someone else's, though, before. I can see a woman. She's got long blond hair and blue eyes. She looks like your mom, but different."

"Do you get a name?"

"Yeah, Jolene? Does that sound right?"

I smiled through my tears and nodded. "That was my mom's mom."

"It was her ring?"

I nodded again.

Andy looked down at the ring. "There's another person, too." He cocked his head to the side. "Ann?"

I nodded again. "My great-grandma on my mom's side."

Andy smiled. "This ring was pilfered."

"What?"

"Five finger discount. Stolen."

I grabbed the ring back from him. "Shut up. No, it wasn't."

"Seriously, Anderson. Your great-grandpa conned it off an old woman at church."

"He did not!" I felt my face grow red with anger.

Andy chuckled. "No worries, we all have our sordid pasts!"

I stared down at the ring and turned it in my hands. Shoving it on my finger, I sat, staring out the window.

"Um, is anyone going to tell us what just happened?" Evie's voice was quiet.

"Her great-grandpa was playing a poker game and won the ring with about fifty bucks one night. I was teasing you, Anderson."

Evie cleared her throat. "I meant, how does he know all of that stuff?"

"He can see things like you could after I touched your soul." I continued to stare out the window. "And we can talk to each other through our thoughts."

The car was quiet for a long time.

"Cool," Tristan said.

I turned at the coldness in his voice. "What's wrong?"

He looked out the window. "Nothing. I'm fine."

"He's feeling left out," Grant said. He reached over to grab my hand. "You three belong to the official club now, and we don't."

"*You* can see what people are feeling now?" Evie asked.

"No, just know what it feels like to be shut out of something." The muscle in Grant's jaw worked.

"Good grief, man," Andy said. "Anderson loves you so much she can't stand it sometimes. She thinks about you all the time and counts down the seconds until she sees you again. Really, it's pretty icky."

"Get out of my head," I snarled.

Grant squeezed my hand, a smile breaking on his face. "I love all that icky stuff."

"Can I get some of that anti-nausea medicine?" Evie asked.

A giggle started in my throat and suddenly I was laughing. My stomach clenched as I lost control, laughter bubbling up from my core. Gale after gale sprouted forth until tears ran down my cheeks. It spread and soon all of us were laughing. It quieted for a minute and then Andy snorted and we all started up again.

The laughter faded the second the car rolled over the last hill and the edge of town came into view. Grant pulled his car off onto the last exit before town and we sat there, the engine idling in the quiet morning.

"Where do we go first?" Grant asked. His knuckles were white as he gripped the steering wheel.

"The quarry. We pick up Andy's truck and then they go to the place we stayed last night. See if they can find anything. We go to Melanie's. Meet back here in two hours."

"Everyone charged?"

We all looked at our phones and nodded.

"Ready?" Grant asked. His eyes flicked up to the rearview and back down again.

I nodded, my teeth clenched.

He put the car in gear and we started rolling toward the town of Culvers Grove and the scariest thing any of us had ever faced.

ADRIA WATERS

CHAPTER 20

Andy's truck took a few minutes to turn over, and then it roared to life with an angry black cloud of exhaust boiling from the tailpipe. He rolled down the window and leaned out.

"Call if you get into any trouble? Don't try to handle anything by yourself."

I nodded. *I promise.*

Andy held my gaze for a moment longer and then rolled up his window and drove away. Grant followed for a bit and then turned the opposite way when the road forked. Gravel crunched under his tires and was the only sound in the car. He shifted when we turned onto a paved road, reaching over to grab my hand with the motion.

"Plan on saying anything?" he asked.

I shook my head. Truth was, now that we were inside the wall, I was draining. Fast. I concentrated on picking up any glimmer of my grandmother. Nothing. The longer we drove, the more frustrated I got. And the more drained. I yawned and leaned my head back onto the headrest.

"Don't try to do too much," Grant said. His hand was warm with reassurance as it held mine.

"I won't." I closed my eyes and allowed the car's motion to relax my muscles. I imagined a warm ball of light passing down each of my shoulders, rolling along the hard knots of stress that were drawing them up to my ears. As I envisioned the light moving down my arms, I felt the car stop.

"We're here," Grant said. "At least, I think we are."

My eyes came open and I looked out onto the town. Nothing moved. No one was out walking. No cars moved down the street. The feeling of isolation grew as Grant nosed his car along Main Street. We passed several houses and businesses as we made our way into town. The businesses were all closed and shutters were drawn.

I glanced over at Grant. "What's going on?" I breathed.

"I don't know."

We crept along the empty street until we reached Melanie's house. Grant put the car in park and turned it off.

"Everything quiet here?" he asked.

I closed my eyes and concentrated. Then, I nodded. "Yeah, I don't feel anything."

"Good. Come on."

He got out and I slid out behind him, not wanting to let go of his hand and the connection I felt. Even though there were no cars, we looked both ways out of habit before crossing the street, and then climbed the steps to Melanie's house. Her driveway had not been shoveled, but then, neither had any of her neighbors'. Knocking snow from our boots, Grant reached out to ring the doorbell.

Silence.

"Try again."

He reached out again and was about to ring the doorbell when he drew his hand back. "Look at that."

I stepped over and saw a sign hanging from her door under the wilted wreath. "No solicitation. We will not be opening the door to protect ourselves from the outbreak." I turned wide eyes to Grant. "The outbreak?"

He shook his head and yanked open the screen door. He raised a fist and banged on the wooden door. "Mrs.

Ingalls, it's Grant and Marissa. We're not sick. We want to talk to you!"

I grabbed his arm. "You're going to scare her."

"We need to talk to her, and the longer we're out here, the longer it has to lock in on your signal."

"I'm not a beacon," I sulked.

Grant banged on the door again. "That's *exactly* what you are. Mrs. Ingalls! Open up, please!"

We stood there for a couple of minutes. I turned and did a mental sweep of the street. Still nothing. Something pulled at me from inside, though, and I had a moment of panic before I remembered that Melanie's husband was in there. The pull was stronger, though, more cognizant. I shrugged the feeling away, but it persisted, pressing against me. *Was Melanie sick? Or...*I didn't want to think about it and reached around Grant to bang on the door myself.

"Melanie! It's Marissa. Johnny's in trouble!"

That did the trick. The curtain in the sidelight moved a bit and a withered face peered out at us.

"Melanie, we need to talk to you. We're not sick. Open up, please?"

She cast a worried glance around us and held up her finger. A moment later, the lock turned and she opened the door. A frailer, paler version of Melanie stood in the foyer, motioning us inside as she slammed the door behind her. She wore a medical mask and her eyes were watery and bloodshot above it.

I reached out to take her hand, but she pulled it back before I made contact.

She motioned to the couch and we sat, not bothering to take off our coats or gloves. I could see Mr. Ingalls snoozing in the recliner, his toe peeking out of a hole in his sock. The feeling intensified now that we were inside and I heard a thump above me from the attic.

"Did you hear that?" I asked.

Melanie shook her head, but I had already noticed her eyes turn upwards.

"What's going on here?" I asked.

"There's been a terrible influenza outbreak," Melanie said, her voice muffled by the mask. "Everyone's sick." She sat down with a grunt. "I think I'm coming down with something. I'm tired something fierce."

"Melanie, my dad is in trouble. I need your help. I need to find my grandma."

Melanie stared at me through watery eyes.

"I don't have time to explain everything. I need you to believe me and tell me where my grandma buried her first child."

Melanie took a deep breath. A thump sounded from upstairs again and her eyes flitted up to the ceiling. "He's buried at Hubbard Cemetery, right outside town. She lost him to Scarlett fever when he was a year old.

Saddest thing I'd ever heard. She was different after that." Her eyes unfocused as she relived a moment from her past. Then they focused on me again. "What kind of trouble is Johnny in?"

I swallowed.

Grant placed his hand over mine. "We don't know. We think there's something here in the town that is really bad and it's pulling spirits to it and using them to make the town sick."

Melanie nodded as if he'd told her that the sky was blue and cake was good. She didn't bat an eye as she looked up at the ceiling again. "That's why I'm keeping Thomas safe up there."

I gasped. "Thomas? He's here?"

"Shhh," she put a finger pulled crooked by arthritis to her lips. "Yes, he's here. I don't know how he got here, but it must have been something we did out at the lake that day." She smiled. "You brought my boy home to me. I can even see him and hear him sometimes." She coughed, her face turning red with effort. "Excuse me." She got up and toddled to the kitchen.

I looked over at Grant. "I didn't do anything. He was already gone when we got there. Sam took him twenty-five years ago."

"Took him where?"

"I don't know. I only saw him disappear into a portal he built. Sam said he was going to help him not be alone."

"You think Sam brought him here?"

"She said he didn't show up until after we were at the lake."

Grant stared at the coffee table. Then he brought his gaze up to me. "What if he brought Thomas here and he was happy. He would have been like your grandparents, just hanging out until…"

I snapped to attention. "Oh my gosh. It's *waking* them up now?"

Grant nodded. "I don't know, but it makes sense if it's gotten strong enough."

Melanie came back into the living room, readjusting her mask.

"What is Thomas doing? When you see him?" I asked.

"I can't really tell. He won't talk to me. He keeps moving boxes around up there. Putting them in a circle."

"Or a portal," Grant breathed in my ear.

I nodded. "Melanie, we have to go. Thank you. And listen, please take care of yourself. Be safe and don't let anyone in."

She nodded, but all of the life and spunk were drained from her and I found myself staring at a shell of a woman.

I reached out, and this time, she let me take her hand. "We'll come back and check on you. I promise."

She let us out and Grant and I stood on the porch, watching as ghosts milled around on the sidewalks.

"Where did they all come from?" Grant whispered.

"I'm the beacon, remember?"

With my words, several ghosts turned their heads and began moving our way. Grant and I ran to the car, slamming the doors closed. The ghosts followed our car as we headed out of town.

"How are we doing on time?" I asked.

He checked his phone. "We have a little over an hour."

"Hubbard Cemetery?"

He nodded. "Let's go."

A few minutes later, we pulled into the narrow driveway of a lonely cemetery. On the outskirts of the town, it was ringed with a black wrought iron fence with spikes along the top in front and a chain link version along the sides and back. I started to get out, but Grant placed a hand on my arm.

"Let me get turned around," he said.

I nodded and waited until he had turned the nose of the car back toward the road. "Smart," I said. I got out and made my way up to the gate. An arch spread over me with Hubbard Cemetery spelled out in iron scrollwork. I passed through, my feet sinking in the snow along the walkway.

"I'll watch out for you," Grant said from the archway. "Do your thing, Ghost Girl."

I tried to smile, but the weight of the sadness and sickness in the town pressed down on me. I shook my head and closed my eyes. "She's not here." *But, she had been.* I opened my eyes and watched as spectral footprints appeared in the snow to my right. *There.* I followed the prints as they moved slowly along the perimeter of the graveyard. I made my way along the fence to my right, stumbling as I passed by a large gravestone that jutted at an angle from the snow-covered ground. The footprints broke from the fence and headed into the middle of the cemetery. I followed them, my breath coming in bursts as I walked in the wake of her emotion. My heart hurt and I felt a familiar emptiness wash over me.

A few feet ahead, the footprints paused and then there was a soft puff of snow as two parallel lines appeared. *She knelt here.* I went forward and crouched next to the memory of my grandmother. In front of me was a small block of stone. I reached out to brush the snow away with my bare hand. There, on the block of stone, was one word. A name: Isaiah. I placed my hand on the cold stone and closed my eyes.

My grandmother, young and full of life. She was sitting in her chair at the farm, a fire blazing in the fireplace as she rocked the little one. She crooned at him, her eyes full of love. Then the image shifted, growing dark around the edges. Now she was standing above his crib, tears streaming down her face. His little body wracked with a horrible rattling sound. She reached down and felt his feverish forehead. The image shifted again and I watched his tiny casket lowered into the ground. My grandparents, dressed in black, held onto one another as the pastor placed a handful of dirt onto the small box.

I opened my eyes, not wanting to see any more.

Don't stop now. You must see what is next.

I drew a shaky breath and closed my eyes again. There was my grandmother again. Now it was nighttime and she was seated beside the fresh dirt of her first son's grave. She reached into the front of her dress and glanced over her shoulder furtively. I watched as she bent over, digging at the dirt near the base of the stone with short, furtive movements. I leaned around her image, aiming for a better look. I was pushed to the side and suddenly I was falling.

I landed in the snow and looked up. Grant stood above me, his hand outstretched. Panic tinged his eyes. He said something and pulled me to my feet. I felt snow creep into my collar and I shivered. I spoke, but my mouth was dry. Swallowing, I tried to climb out of the fogginess. The day had taken on a muted tone. The sun was still out and glittering on the snow, but the day had lost all of its brightness.

He pulled on my hand again, trying to catch my line of vision.

Vision.

She was trying to show me something.

"I-I have to see…" I started to kneel down again, but Grant locked his grasp on my arm.

I turned to look at him again, everything moving in slow motion.

"…we…"

I concentrated on his mouth, on the movements of his lips as he formed the words.

"…have…"

The sound reached my ears an eternity after his mouth made them and the sensation was disconcerting. I shook my head again, the cobwebs in my mind falling to the side with the motion. I looked up again, locking eyes with Grant. Everything around me snapped into clarity.

"We have company," he said, jerking his head over his shoulder.

I leaned around him, and my breath caught in my throat.

At least a hundred spirits circled us in the cemetery, moving toward us in slow, jerky movements. A cloud of black smoke skimmed along the top of them, watching us with a hungry ferocity as it touched a ghost and then hopped along to the next, around the circle. I felt icicles run through my veins as I realized that we were trapped. Grant realized it at the same time I did and he put himself in front of me, trying to shield me from the tightening circle. I glanced over at the entrance, his car mere yards beyond. The circle closed in.

There's no way out.

CHAPTER 21

The circle of spirits closed around the cemetery. Grant and I stood back to back, turning slowly as they approached. I saw Amalie, her hair caked to her head and her eyes vacant. I called out to her, but she didn't answer. *She's too far gone.*

I took a step back and my feet met with open air. Looking down, I saw the ground swirling around me. Grant lost his balance and pulled me toward him as he moved to a higher piece of ground. I stared at the swirling dirt.

"They're making a portal," I said, my voice even and devoid of emotion.

Grant grabbed my hand. "We can make a run for it."

I shook my head and let my hand fall from his. My head hurt and I was tired. "The smoke would get to us before we made it to your car."

"We have to do something!"

I leaned against the gravestone behind me. It was cold on my back.

"Marissa! We have to get your dad out!"

The vestiges of apathy fell away and I snapped to attention.

Andy, we need help. Now. Hubbard Cemetery.

I didn't know how far away they were, but we wouldn't last more than a few minutes. I had to do something. Planting my feet into the ground, I stood up straight and focused all of my energy on the small piece of earth where Grant and I stood. I breathed slowly and evenly as I concentrated on making the ground stop swirling. I reached out for Grant and pulled him into the eye of the storm. In here, it was quiet. The sloshing sound of the ghosts approaching was drowned out by the silence of our little cocoon of peace. The ground grew solid under our feet and I held onto Grant, never allowing my concentration to waver.

"They're getting closer," Grant whispered.

"I know," I breathed. "Hold on."

Andy, you have to hurry.

I listened for any hint that he had heard me. Any indication that he was coming.

Nothing.

I opened my eyes for a moment and saw that the circle had grown tighter. The spirits were inside the fence now, drawing into a tight circle, almost shoulder to shoulder at this point. I closed my eyes again and held onto the solid ground. *You can't take me like this. When I meet you, it's going to be on my terms.* I let that thought course through me and then I heard an engine.

I opened my eyes and saw Andy's truck fishtail as it rocketed up the driveway. Holding my breath, I looked at Grant. "We're going to have to move fast. I can only hold on for a little longer."

I'm here, Anderson. Oh, crap. You guys really stepped in it, didn't you?

I smiled to myself.

Yeah. We need your help. Want to test out that target theory?

The truck pulled up next to Grant's car and my friends swung out, their feet planted in the snow. It would have been an epic moment had I not been so scared. Tristan started Grant's car, then climbed back into Andy's truck, waiting as Evie and Andy approached the cemetery.

"Hey, guys! We came to party!"

At the sound of Andy's voice, a few spirits around the edge turned. The smoke moved to them, beckoning their attention back to the center of the circle, toward us.

Do it again. I took a centering breath. "Grant, when Andy gets their attention, we're going to run through the opening. I'll make a path."

"You can do that?" he asked.

I nodded. *Liar.*

My stomach twisting with uncertainty, I pushed my influence out, testing it. The solid ground extended a few feet toward the spirits.

"Hey! Over here!" Evie shouted. Her voice shook, though, and her face was pale.

"We have some really cool souls over here! Seriously, it's a two for one deal!"

The same spirits turned again, this time breaking from the circle. The smoke moved to them, caressing their faces with gossamer hands, attempting to turn their attention.

Keep it up.

"Super cool souls here! Get your super cool souls!" Andy and Evie linked arms and moved toward the ghosts that had broken off from the circle.

As they moved, a space about three feet wide opened up and I saw my chance. The smoke was trying to get the circle to close again and I knew it would only be distracted for a few seconds.

"Now!" I hissed, pushing the solid ground out from my feet. It created a bridge across the swirling ground and Grant and I darted along it. We jumped through the space between the spirits and landed in a snow bank on the other side. Something grabbed my ankle and I turned to look back. My foot was mired in the swirling ground, pulled down toward the abyss below. My stomach cramped with the realization that this portal was powerful enough to pull a living person into it. I gritted my teeth and jerked away. As I did, I twisted my ankle, falling down and taking Grant with me.

We were out, but now the spirits' attention was back on us again.

"Over here!" Andy shouted.

"Here!" Evie cried.

It was no use. The smoke swung around and regarded us, a sinister darkness spreading through it. The spirits began moving toward us as Grant got up and yanked me to my feet. His face was gray.

I cried out as I put my weight down on my leg. My ankle felt like it was on fire. "I can't. My ankle's messed up. Go on!" I pushed him away.

Always the martyr, huh, Anderson?

Shut up. Get out and get somewhere safe.

No dice, kid.

Andy broke from Evie and ran toward us, arms spread wide. "Ghostie in the circle, one, two, three. Ghostie in the circle, come get me!"

No!

Better run, Anderson. This is only going to buy you a couple of seconds.

I grabbed for Grant's hand and ignoring the pain searing through my leg, I practically pulled him down the hill toward his car. When we reached the doors, I took a moment to look behind me. Evie ran toward the truck, her eyes wild with fear.

Andy pounded steps behind, his mouth stretched into a wide grin. "Got their attention now!"

I watched for a second in horror as the spirits funneled through the gate, filtering out onto the snowy hill. The smoke jettisoned out, reaching for Andy's retreating figure. I wasn't sure if it was my viewpoint, but it looked like the smoke was only inches from touching him.

Run!

What do you think I'm doing?

Do it faster!

He winked at me as he passed and jumped into the passenger seat of the truck. I slid into Grant's car and yanked the door closed as he hit the gas. The car slid to the side and then caught traction. Grant barreled out the gravel drive with Tristan right behind us.

"We have to go back," I said.

Grant tossed me a look that was nothing short of incredulous. "Please tell me you're kidding."

I was quiet, pressing my thoughts back behind the truck, keeping the spirits at bay as we rolled away. Tears streamed down my face as I tried to find a comfortable position that didn't put any pressure on my ankle.

By the time we reached the highway, the sun was high in the sky, melting the layers of snow in its wake. Grant's car broke through the invisible wall and the pain disappeared in my ankle. I looked down and pushed my boot off with my other foot, prepared to see a red and swollen ankle. When I pulled my sock down, though, my ankle was perfectly fine. I tentatively moved it from side to side, gritting my teeth. Nothing. It was *fine*. I put my boot back on.

Grant pulled onto the exit ramp and stopped the car. He leaned back in the seat, resting his head against the headrest. He closed his eyes and took a few deep breaths as Tristan nosed the truck to the shoulder behind us.

"Had enough yet?" I asked quietly.

Grant didn't open his eyes. He took another deep breath and then sat up and turned to me. His gaze was unwavering. "Marissa, I was so afraid I was going to lose you back there." He reached out and placed a hand on my cheek, wiping away a tear with his thumb.

"I-I'm fine. My ankle doesn't hurt anymore at all. How's your stomach?"

He lifted his shirt. No sign of any blood. "I'm good."

I heard the truck doors slam behind us. A second later, my door opened and Andy reached in and grabbed my arm, pulling me out onto the side of the road.

"What are you doing?" I asked.

He took a long look at me, his face serious. Once he established that I was in one piece, he pulled me to him in a huge hug. I felt his heart beating a million miles an hour and his breathing was ragged.

"Don't do that again," he said as he let me go.

"Thanks for saving our butts, man," Grant said from across the roof of the car.

Andy left his arm hanging around my shoulders and nodded. "Yeah, you would've done the same for me."

"Probably," Grant smiled.

"That was pretty intense," Evie said as she approached. "I didn't think we were going to make it out of there."

"Did you all find anything at the house we stayed at last night?"

Evie's eyes darted to Andy. She chewed on her bottom lip.

"What?" I asked. I moved away from Andy to turn and face him. *You know I'll find out anyway.*

He nodded. "She'll hear it in my thoughts anyway," he said to Evie.

"Fine. When we went out there, we got about a half mile away before we saw the smoke." She paused for a moment. "It was burned down, St. Louis."

"By what?" I thought back to that night. *Had we forgotten to put out the fire in the fireplace? Had we burned down the house?*

"I poured snow on the embers before we left yesterday morning. There wasn't anything hot left anyway because someone was out traipsing through the snow talking to Native Americans and couldn't be bothered to throw a log on the fire." Andy winked at me.

I narrowed my eyes at him. "Burned down? Nothing left?"

Evie nodded. "I'm assuming because you were out at the cemetery that you talked to Melanie?"

I filled her in on our conversation with Melanie and the fact that Thomas was upstairs building a portal.

"It's waking them up now," she breathed. It wasn't a question.

"I think so."

"Marissa wants to go back to the cemetery," Grant said.

Evie and Andy turned to look at me as a semi-truck barreled past us on the ramp. The driver stared at us as he drove by.

"Please tell me that I didn't hear him correctly," Andy said. "That's a death sentence, Anderson."

"I saw something there. I saw my grandmother bury something near the baby's headstone."

"She was there?" Evie asked.

I shook my head. "No, but her memory was. She buried something right after he died."

"So, let me get this straight, Anderson. You want to go back to the place where we were chased by a gaggle of bloodthirsty spirits to dig up a baby's grave." He tilted his head. "That's a little macabre, even for you, don't you think?"

I glared at him.

"A portal opened up, too," Grant said.

They swung their gazes to him.

He shut the door and came around the car. "It almost sucked us in, but Marissa was able to keep us from being taken."

Evie and Andy looked from Grant to me.

"How?" Evie asked.

I shrugged. "I don't really know. All I did was concentrate on making the ground solid under our feet. I made a bridge for us to run across. I wasn't sure it was going to work when I did it." I glanced sheepishly at Grant.

"I knew you didn't know what you were doing." He winked.

"But, if she hadn't made the ground solid, what would have happened?" Evie asked. "I mean, it can't pull, um, living people through, right?" She shifted from foot to foot.

"It sure felt like it could've swallowed us whole," Grant said finally.

I nodded. "It pulled my foot. That's why I fell."

"But you're, well, you're alive. I thought it could only take spirits." Evie's eyes were hopeful. She bit her bottom lip and squeaked out, "Right?"

"It's getting really strong," Andy said.

"It's got a lot of ghosts." Grant leaned against the side of the car. "I think it gains strength from them."

I took a deep breath. "If we go back in there, what are the chances the ghosts are still at the cemetery?"

Andy regarded me. "Like a thousand and ten percent."

I sighed again. "I don't know what to do here. I wish I could find my grandma."

"Come look at this," Tristan's voice came from the back of the truck.

I hadn't noticed he had walked away. We all rounded the truck and stood looking down at the bed of the pickup where Tristan had laid the copy of the cave system. "Check this out." He turned on his phone and a light projected onto the map. "We need to block out the sun."

"On it," Andy said. He peeled off his coat and he and Grant took a side each, canopying the coat over the phone and map. When they did, enough sunlight was drowned out to allow the image he was projecting to cover the cave map.

"Is that...Culvers Grove?" I asked, squinting.

Tristan smiled. "Yep. My grandma got me this phone case projector last Christmas and I haven't had a reason to use it yet. Well, until now anyways."

"Taking my job as the tech guy?" Andy teased.

"Look, here's the courthouse." He pointed to the center of the town. Roads overlaid the cave system that spiraled out from the center like the spokes of a giant wagon wheel. "And here's Sarah's house. You notice anything?"

I leaned in, peering at the map. Slowly, I shook my head. "Um, I don't know what I'm looking for."

"You're looking for a spoke of the cave system."

I leaned in again until my nose was almost touching the map. "I don't see one."

"Exactly. Here, hold this," he said to Evie. He handed the phone to her and helped her adjust it. "There, now don't move it." Tristan glanced at me. "This is a dead area. From here," he dragged his finger along the road that Amalie's house was on to the highway, down to the creek that ran along the east side of the town and then back to the road in a large triangle. "This whole area is clear of any of the cave's main arteries or tributaries."

I looked closer. "There's no way for the spirits to get to us there."

He smiled. "I mean, they could eventually walk there from one of the other entrances, but I don't think that the BB's reach is quite that powerful yet."

"That's an awfully big gamble to take." Evie's face was grim.

"Think about it. They couldn't follow us very far from the quarry. They had to stop at the edge of the road the other night. I think they go in and out through an entrance and then have to stay pretty close to the cave system. Here," he dug around in his messenger bag. He brought out two black magnets. "Anyone have a piece of paper?"

Andy let his side of the coat dip for a second as he opened the toolbox. He handed a piece of paper to Tristan and then held up the coat again.

"Thanks. Hold this." He handed me the paper and I held it stretched between my hands. He placed one of the magnets on top of the paper. "Watch." He put the other one under the paper and there was a small clap as the magnets snapped together through the sheet of paper. He slid the bottom magnet around, making the top magnet dance across the surface. He took the paper from me. "See what I mean? If it's using these spirits like puppets, they can only travel as far as *it* can."

"They may be able to travel above ground, but they're still tied to the cave system underneath," Grant said.

Tristan nodded. "So, this area here is completely safe. For now. It might be the last safe place in the whole town."

"Then, that's where my grandma is."

Tristan smiled. "That's what I was thinking. You want to try asking her first what she buried before we risk our lives going back to the cemetery?"

I took a deep breath. "Let's go in and find my grandma."

CHAPTER 22

After filling the vehicles with gas and taking a refresher of all of our medications, we climbed back into the truck and car and crossed the overpass to head back into town.

Grant was quiet as he hit the highway. His hand was holding mine as he shifted. Then he placed it on my leg, fingers intertwined through mine.

"You know you don't have to do this, right?"

He smiled and brought my hand to his lips. "You know you don't have to keep asking me that, right?"

I sighed and settled back into the seat. "I don't get you."

He chuckled. "Me? What's to get?"

"Why me?" I asked quietly.

He chuckled again, but the sound died in his throat when he glanced over at me. "Oh, you're serious?"

"Don't make fun of me."

"I'm not. I can't believe I have to keep answering this question."

"And I can't believe this whole thing keeps getting worse and worse. I mean, at what point are you going to say that you've had enough?"

"Is that what you're afraid of? That I'm going to at some point look at you and say, well, it's been real, but I'm going to jet because this has gotten a little too inconvenient for me?"

I nodded, a lump growing in my throat. "I understand why they're with me on this," I said as I glanced behind us at Andy's truck. "I mean, we're the only real family Evie's ever had and Andy and Tristan would follow her into the fire because they're her friends. Mine, too." I wiped my hand over my face. I was babbling. "What I can't figure out is why you are putting up with all of this."

"Suffice it to say that I am in love with you. In fact, I have been since the moment you opened up your back door looking like you'd been attacked by a green swamp monster." He squeezed my hand. "Marissa, I love you, but I am getting tired of having this conversation."

My stomach lurched. We crossed through the barrier and I felt my energy start to drain.

"…you."

I shook my head. "Sorry?"

"I said that I want you to stop pushing me away and let me love you. Do you think you can do that?"

I took a deep breath and tried to stop the hemorrhage of my energy as we drove toward my great grandmother's house. "I will try. I don't want you to feel obligated."

He laughed out loud at that one. "I have never felt obligated to you. You're a good person, Marissa. You put absolutely everything on the line to help people. Now, will you sit there and let people help you for a change without questioning their intentions?"

I smiled, my eyes closing of their own will. "I'm tired."

"Then sleep, my Paranormal Princess. I'll let you know when we get there."

I pulled my coat over me and buried into the warm cocoon. We had only gone a few miles when I heard Grant downshift and curse under his breath.

My eyes flew open. "What's wrong?"

He jutted his chin toward the road in front of him. There, standing shoulder to shoulder was a line of about twenty-five spirits. The smoke danced along, snaking through their legs, its movements jerky and almost daring us to come closer. Grant pulled as close to the edge of the road as he dared. Andy stopped behind him.

"What do we do now?" he asked.

I turned around in my seat. *Any ideas?*

Tristan's already got the map out. Follow us.

"Follow Andy," I said to Grant.

"How long is that going to last?" He smiled as he put the car in reverse and turned around, following the truck.

We snaked along several roads until I was almost completely lost. As we went up a long, twisty gravel road, Andy's brake lights came on. Grant stopped.

It's a no go here, too.

The reverse lights came on and Grant waited until Andy passed by on his left before turning the car around.

We tried three more routes, but we were cut off at each one. Grant and I followed the truck as it wound its way back the way we came. My phone buzzed. It was Evie.

"Hey. Tristan has one more idea, but we're going to have to leave Grant's car behind. You think he'll be okay with that?"

I glanced over at Grant. "Yeah. Tell me what to do."

"Meet us at the auto parts store in town."

"Seriously?"

Grant looked over at me.

I covered the speaker. "Tristan wants us to go into town."

Grant shook his head. "No way. We're safer out here in the open."

I relayed the message to Evie.

She was quiet for a second and I could see her turning from Tristan to Andy in the truck. Finally, she came back on. "Pull over here." The phone went dead.

Grant pulled over next to the truck and I rolled down my window.

Andy rolled his down, too. "The only other way to get in is straight through the barrier at the top point of the triangle. We're going to have to do some off-roading, though. In this snow, we'll need to put some chains on my truck. The only place that has them is the auto parts store. You ever put them on?"

Grant nodded. "Yeah, I used to help my dad put them on his truck."

"Good. You and Tristan go into town, put on the chains and we'll take your car and meet you by the old abandoned gas station on highway eleven. You know where that is?"

Grant nodded again, his lips drawn tight. "Yeah, I know where that is. Are you guys going to be safe?" His eyes shifted to me.

"We'll be outside the barrier, so yes. When you and Tristan get back, we can drive my truck in using an old road to the property that Tristan found."

I watched the conversation flow over me as if I was watching a tennis match. "Wait a minute."

Oh, I figured you'd have something to say about all this.

"Shut up," I said. "I'm not sending you two into town alone. What if something happens?"

"It's the only way, Anderson."

Grant touched my arm. "Tristan and I are the only ones who don't have a…"

"…great big fat target on their butts," Andy supplied.

"Maybe we can walk from the barrier to the house?"

"It's about three miles from that point to the house. You feeling up to a hike through a foot of snow?"

I sat back in the seat. The truth was, even the effort of holding up my end of this conversation had me feeling as if I could curl up for a three-day nap. I shook my head.

"We need to get going," Evie said. She was looking out the back window of the truck.

I followed her gaze and saw the line of spirits walking our way.

"It's up to you, Anderson. We won't do anything you don't want to, but I don't see another way. It's not going to let us get anywhere in this town."

I looked over at Grant. "You're going to be safe?"

He smiled and reached out to cup my face in his hands. "We'll be fine. Don't worry."

I turned to look at Andy. "Fine."

Andy's eyes took on a sad wistfulness and I felt instantly guilty. After all, he loved Tristan like I loved Grant. He was as worried as I was.

They'll be fine. I tried to reassure him.

You suck at lying even in your head, Anderson.

Andy climbed out of his truck and Evie slid out behind him and got into the backseat of Grant's car. Tristan took his post behind the wheel of the truck and moved the seat forward. He gripped the steering wheel as Andy closed the door.

"Second gear's a little tricky," Grant said. He smiled at me. "We'll be fine. We have our phones."

"Can't you grab the chains and meet us?" I asked. "Or, let's drive into Chillicothe and go to the auto shop there?" I was grasping at straws.

He grabbed my hands in his. "We'll need to use their tools to get the chains on. Going to Chillicothe will only eat up another day. Your dad doesn't have that long, does he?"

The mention of my dad galvanized me and I nodded. "He's already been down too long." I leaned over the middle console and kissed Grant's lips softly. "Be careful, please."

He kissed me again. "I promise."

Cold air blew in through the door as he opened it and stepped out. I climbed over the middle and sat down behind the wheel as Andy folded his long frame into the seat I vacated. Andy's truck pulled out onto the road. We followed for several miles and then came to a stop sign that was faded to a magenta color. It rose from the ground at a jaunty angle, its white outline riddled with rust. Here, Tristan turned left toward town. Grant rolled his window down and raised a hand in a wave. My eyes filled with tears as I turned right and headed out to the highway.

"They'll be fine, right?" I asked.

No one answered me as we drove down the road, the tires humming on the asphalt. My stomach roiled as I got further and further from Grant, and I kept my hands locked on the steering wheel, afraid that if I let up, I would fall apart. Tears burned my eyes as I hit the highway and headed out through the barrier. I expected to feel better, but my stomach was still a mess even as we made our way to highway eleven.

At one point, Evie reached up to place a hand on our shoulders. I bit my bottom lip against the emotion that welled up.

"Everything's going to be fine, you guys. Right?"

"Yeah," Andy said, his voice shaking.

I nodded and kept my eyes on the road.

By the time we reached the abandoned gas station on the side of the two-lane highway, it was late in the afternoon and the buttery rays of sun filtered through the tall trees rising up along the side of the road. I maneuvered Grant's car behind the gas station between an old rusted out delivery truck and a trash bin, hiding it from sight from any passing cars. I turned it off and the silence bore down on us. I took my phone from my pocket and laid it on my leg.

Fifteen minutes later, my phone buzzed, stirring me from my thoughts. I looked down. "It's Grant!"

I brought up the text. *Check this out.* The outline of three photos appeared with a little circle showing their pending status. The signal out here was terrible and I held the phone up to the roof of the car. A ping indicated that one of the photos had come through. I brought my phone down and swiped the screen. A photo appeared. It showed the quiet street that ran to the front of the auto parts store. No ghosts wandered the sidewalks. The next picture showed the auto parts store. It was empty. No ghosts. I let out my breath. The last photo was still loading.

"It looks like they're safe," I said. My phone binged again. This picture was taken from the front of the auto parts store and showed the yard of the courthouse in the distance. Scattered on the lawn were more ghosts than I could count. I brought my hand up to my mouth.

We're safe. They haven't noticed us yet. See you soon. Luvu.

I rolled the word around in my mind. *Yet.* I passed the phone to Andy.

"They have no reason to pay any attention to them," he said, but I could see the tension pulling at his mouth. "They'll be fine."

I nodded. "Yeah, they'll be fine."

The shadows of the trees lengthened, dropping the temperature as our car settled into the darkness. Andy and I climbed into the backseat with Evie. We took off our coats and zipped them together to create a long blanket that we spread over ourselves. I tucked myself into a small ball and leaned into Evie's warmth. She reached over, smoothed my hair behind my ear, and then pulled my hat down over my head. I let my head rest on her shoulder, comforted by her even breathing. My eyes drooped and I shivered once and then sleep finally won the battle I had been fighting with all afternoon.

It felt like only minutes had passed when I felt Evie shaking me awake.

"St. Louis! We fell asleep!"

I sat up, my breath hanging in the freezing interior of the car. I scrambled over the seat and jammed the key into the ignition. The car roared to life, blowing frigid air through the vents at me. My eyes watered and I turned the fan down, wiping at my eyes.

"How long were we out?" Andy asked, his teeth chattering.

I tried to focus on the clock on my phone, but the water in my eyes made everything blurry. I wiped at them again and stared down at my phone. The clock said it was ten thirty.

I looked up at Andy. "Do you have any messages from Tristan?"

He looked at his phone and then up at me. *No.*

I heard panic in his answer. I hit dial and put the phone to my ear. Straight to voicemail. Which meant Grant's phone had either run out of battery or he had it turned off or… I didn't want to go down that line of thought. I texted him, my fingers flying over the screen. *Call me.*

Andy had dialed Tristan's number as well. He put the phone down and shook his head. "Straight to voicemail."

I put the car in gear and turned to look over my shoulder as we reversed.

"What are you doing?" Evie asked.

"I'm going to find them," I answered, trying not to let the edge in my voice carry.

She placed a hand on my shoulder. "How far do you think we'll get, St. Louis? All of us together are a huge beacon. We can't go in there or it will find us."

My eyes filled with tears. "What am I supposed to do?" My voice wavered. I was dangerously close to losing it.

Evie's hand pressed down. "We wait. What if they get here and we're gone?"

"We can text them. Let them know we went into town to look for them. I don't know!" I didn't mean to be yelling at her, but I couldn't help it.

"Give it one more hour?" she said quietly.

"You wouldn't be saying that if it was someone you loved," I spat. "If it was *Sam*."

Evie blinked, but regained her composure. She leveled her gaze at me. "I would do what he told me to do. I would wait because I knew he was going to be safe and he would come for me like he promised."

I turned on Andy. "What about you? Do you have any thoughts on this or are you content with going along with whatever she says?" The tears were streaming unabated down my face now and my hands shook on the steering wheel.

"Me? Well, I would stay right where I was because someone is coming."

"What are you talking about?"

He nodded his head to the front of the car. I spun around.

There, from the front of the building were two beams of bright light, shining into the dark forest beyond, mist rising and dancing in the light.

CHAPTER 23

I heard a car door open and close and then the headlight beams were broken up by a shadow. I turned the car off and killed the lights.

It's the Po-Po!

I brushed Andy's attempt at a joke off. I was still seething. The figure came around the corner of the building and I heard the back door open. Andy darted across the lot and gathered Tristan in a bear hug. I opened my door and got out, my legs shaky. I watched the corner of the building for another figure. A figure that would walk around and brush his hair out of his eyes. A figure that would smile his crooked smile at me, hold me, and kiss the top of my head. The figure never came, though. My throat constricted as Evie got out and stood next to me. She spread my coat over my shoulders, and then her arm twined through mine.

Andy turned and looked back at me. The side of Tristan's face was bathed in the light of the truck. His eyes were watery and his face was pulled taut with worry.

"Come on, St. Louis," Evie said, urging me forward.

Dread ran through my body, the muscles in my core clenching painfully. Tears sprang to my eyes again. I couldn't get my legs to work.

What's wrong? Even in my head, my voice was plaintive and small.

Andy came toward me. *Hang in there, kid.*

Andy, where's Grant?

He approached with a light tread, quietly, not making eye contact. He looked at Evie, his lips drawn tight. "Get everything out of the car and lock it up." When he got to me, he took my hands. *Come on.*

My world began to crack around the edges. Breathing was hard and I gulped down a few huge breaths of air.

Andy put his arm around me and led me to Tristan. Tristan reached out to me, but dropped his hand in a move that read of complete exhaustion. "I don't know what happened, Marissa."

As I rounded the corner, I saw the truck. A figure was sitting, silhouetted in the passenger seat.

"Grant!" I broke from Andy's grasp and ran toward the truck.

"Anderson! Stay back!"

I ignored him and ran to the truck, my cold hands grappling with the door handle. Grant sat inside, staring straight out the window, his face drawn into a grimace of pain.

"Grant!" I yanked hard on the door and it finally came open. "Grant!" I reached in and touched him. He was stiff and cold, unmoving under my hands.

Andy was behind me then, pulling me away.

I turned and struck out at him, my fist making contact with his chest.

He gathered me to him and held me against him as I fought, his voice quiet in my ear. "Tristan and Grant went to the cemetery to dig up whatever you saw your grandmother bury. They found something and Grant picked it up. The ghosts were starting to circle again so they ran for the truck. They beat it out of there and everything was fine until they crossed out of town. As soon as they went through the barrier, Tristan said Grant cried out and went into a convulsion. He stopped the truck and tried to get the thing out of his hand, but he had a death grip on it." He took a deep breath, his chest rising. "Marissa, you can't touch it. We don't know what it is."

I pulled away from him. "I have to try. Look at him!"

"I'm so sorry," Tristan said from behind Andy.

Evie came around the side of the building and stopped. She took in the scene in front of her. "He's in pain. There's something," she tilted her head to the side, "*colorless* in his hands."

"What is it?" I asked.

She shook her head and came closer. "It's like a void of some sort. Um," she shook her head, "I don't know how to describe it, but I've seen something like it before."

"Where?" I shouted at her.

She glanced over at me, the picture of calm.

I seriously considered throttling her. "Evie!"

"On you. It looks like you sometimes."

That was it. If she wasn't going to make any more sense than that, I wasn't going to wait anymore. Grant was hurting and I had to help him. I darted back to the truck and grabbed his hands.

"Grant, it's Marissa. I want you to let go of this, okay?" My voice shook. I felt the group gather closer around me.

Grant turned his head and looked at me. A single tear escaped, sliding down his cheek. His eyes finally focused through the pain and he nodded slowly. He allowed me to pry his fingers away from the object. I looked down. Lying in his blistered palm was a necklace. The charm was a tarnished gold with filigree and roses carved into it. A chain fell from it, intertwined between his fingers.

I licked my lips. Concentrating, I reached down and picked up the chain, pulling it from his grip. He cried out as the charm left his hands with a sizzle. I stared at the filigree burned into his palm like a brand. He leaned back in the seat, with his eyes squeezed shut and his body shaking as he held his hand up in front of him.

I gripped the chain between my fingers, the necklace spinning in the air in a circle.

"Here," Evie said from behind me.

I turned around and she held her coat out.

"Drop it in here."

I held the necklace over the coat and let it drop.

Evie wrapped it up and winced, drawing a hissing breath in between her teeth. She looked up at me. "I can feel it burning my hands even through the material."

I took the bundle from her and held it in front of me. I didn't feel any burning, but I felt completely numb from the neck down anyway. Grant was hurt. Again. And it was my fault. Again.

"Put it in here, Anderson." Andy held open the toolbox in the bed of his truck.

I nodded and placed the coat into the box. Andy slammed it shut.

Get in the truck.

I nodded again and got in, scooting Grant over a bit so I could close the door behind me. He held his hands up and I could see angry welts rising up on his palms. I remembered how much it had hurt when I touched Evie's spirit's hand when she was in a coma. Evie and Tristan climbed in next and wedged themselves into the middle as Andy got in behind the steering wheel. He put the truck in gear and started to drive it around the gas station.

"Where are you going?" I snapped. "We have to take him to the hospital."

Andy stopped the truck.

Grant shook his head. "I'm fine."

Andy started rolling again.

"Uh, no, your hands are burned. You're definitely *not* fine. Andy. Hospital. Now."

Andy stopped the truck.

"No way. How can I be your hero if you run me to the hospital for a little burn?"

I took a deep breath. "You *can't* go back in there. What's going to happen to your hands when we pass through the barrier? Remember your scratches?"

"It didn't burn me until we left town."

I sat staring at him.

Andy looked around the others in the truck and raised his eyebrows. "Dead great-grandmother's house or hospital, Anderson. Make a choice. I'm getting whiplash over here."

You're making a joke? Really? What's wrong with you? Don't you have any compassion?

Grant's voice broke me from my berating of Andy. "Listen, I feel better already now that it's out of my hands. Look," he held his hands up. The palms were red, but the welts and blisters were fading already. "I'll be fine, I promise."

"That's what you said when you and Tristan left earlier," I mumbled.

He smiled. "Dead great-grandmother's house, Andy."

CHAPTER 24

Two miles into the dark field, Grant's hands were almost back to normal. He pulled me onto his lap, allowing a little more room for Andy to move as he negotiated the snowy path.

I looked down at his palms for the hundredth time. "I don't understand."

"I don't think it was supposed to leave the town," Evie said.

"What's with you tonight anyway?" I asked. "You've said hardly anything at all and every time you do, it's to drop this super calm Zen knowledge on us."

She smiled. "I feel really centered for some reason today. I mean, I feel like we have a mission and we know what we're going to do. The hard part was making the plan. Now, we just have to follow it."

I looked at Grant as if to say, see, that's what I'm talking about.

He smiled and leaned in to kiss my cheek. The truck hit an enormous dip in the road and the kiss ended up somewhere on my shoulder.

"Sorry, guys," Andy mumbled as the shocks squeaked through another dip in the road.

I chuckled, and then paused.

"What's wrong?" Evie asked.

"Something you said about feeling centered. I feel that way instead of drained this time. You know, when we passed through the barrier. It's weird." I looked down at Grant's hands again. Then, I grabbed one and brought it close to my face. I ran a finger along his palm gently. "Does that hurt?"

He smiled and moved under me as we bumped along. "No, but it tickles."

"Your hands are fine. Tristan, how do you feel?"

"I still feel awful about what happened earlier. I mean, I didn't know what to do. I'm sorry I couldn't help you, Grant."

"It wasn't your fault. I'm glad you weren't holding it when we drove out of town. We'd be in a ditch somewhere for sure."

I reached over and touched Tristan's knee. "No, I mean, how do you *feel*?"

He shook his head. "I mean, I'm pretty tired, but otherwise, I feel a lot better."

"No coughing?"

"Not for a while, I guess. Not since we got back in the truck anyway."

"Andy? Any nausea?"

"Nope. Starving, though. We still have those granola bars, right?"

"Do you think being away from the cave system is making us all feel better this time?"

The truck was quiet.

Evie finally spoke up. "It makes sense."

"It feels like it did when we were in Chillicothe, right?"

She nodded. "Hey, what's that?" She pointed out the front.

I followed her gesture and squinted against the darkness shrouding the field around us. There was a grove of trees ahead, and from between the trunks were pinpricks of warm light. "Are those…windows?"

"Looks like," Evie said, "that's Sarah's house?"

"It has to be. There's nothing else out here." My mind reeled. *Was there someone in the house?* There was no way there was any electricity still running to that old house. It had long been abandoned and was a shell of a house the last time we were there. "It doesn't make sense."

"And, what about any of this does, Anderson?"

I shook my head, and continued to stare out the window as we approached, the pinpricks of light growing into squares. Figures moved around inside, shadows blocking out the light.

"Do you guys see that?" I whispered.

Grant nodded and hugged me to him. "We see it."

We rounded the trees and Andy's headlights spilled onto the house as he pulled in and stopped in front of it. There was an audible gasp from everyone in the truck as we sat there, staring out at the impossible.

In the grove of trees sat a whitewashed Victorian house. The shutters were black and the scalloped details near the roof were painted a pretty mauve color. Light poured from the house and small tea lights blazed from Mason jars strung along the ceiling and railing of the porch. The balcony above the porch, which had been about to fall in on itself the last time we were here, stood straight and solid, the Adirondack chairs flanked by lush green ferns. Rose bushes hugged the front porch and lilacs in bloom rose up along the corners of the house.

I blinked and pulled at the door handle of the truck. It opened and I braced myself for the frigid winter air. Instead, a warm, honeysuckle-scented breeze lilted through my hair. I stepped out of the truck and stood staring up at the house. It was beautiful and I found myself smiling as I shrugged out of my coat. Everyone else climbed out of the truck without a word.

"You guys are all seeing this, right?" I breathed.

"Yep." Evie pulled her hat off, her black curls spreading out in a frizzy halo around her face. "We're seeing it, St. Louis."

The front door opened and my grandma stepped out onto the porch. She was wearing her apron and she had a smile painted on her face.

"Well, there you all are! We thought maybe you'd gotten lost!"

Faces appeared in the doorway, men and women peering out at us from the foyer. Then, they spilled out onto the porch behind my grandma.

"You all hungry? I have some biscuits and gravy on the stove."

That was all it took. Andy went sprinting up the steps and he was enveloped in the people who swept him inside. Evie, Grant, and Tristan followed.

I stood there a moment longer, staring at my grandma. "What is this?" I asked.

She pointed her wooden spoon at me. "This here is a family reunion, and you're late, little miss."

I started toward the porch and she held up her hand.

"Aren't you planning to bring in that bundle in the back of your friend's truck?"

CHAPTER 25

I walked through the house, the bundle of Evie's coat held gingerly in my arms. I could hear voices from the dining room in the back. Laughter, too. Standing in the middle of the living room, I took it all in. The house was as it must have been in the past, overlaid against the backdrop of the aging home. Broken boards jutted up through the floor that was covered in a thick woven rug. Couches flanked the walls that were bright with the wallpaper I could see peeling beneath. I shook my head and closed my eyes.

Suddenly, my grandma's voice was close to my ear. "It's a bit disconcerting at first, but you'll get used to it."

I opened my eyes. "Is it…real?"

She smiled with a tinge of sadness. "It's as real as any of us are." She brushed flour from her hands onto her apron. "Come on in. I'm sure you're hungry."

My stomach growled in response. I looked down at the bundle in my arms. "What should I do with this?"

She nodded at the credenza. "Set it there." When I hesitated, she placed her hand on my arm. Warmth and energy spread like electricity through my body. "Honey, it's been waiting for over a hundred years. It'll keep a few more minutes."

I placed the coat where she directed. She closed the glass door and led me into the dining room.

It was a bright happy room. A chandelier hung above the large table, dainty bulbs showering the group sitting below in a warm glow. The table was full of food spread out on the white linen tablecloth. Biscuits, gravy, bacon, sausage, jams, jellies, scrambled eggs, and cheese fritters. My eyes rqved over the food, my stomach cramping uncomfortably.

"Have a seat, dear?" A man nodded to the open seat next to him. His hair was brown and slicked back and he wore a white shirt and suspenders. Something about him was somehow off and familiar all at the same time, but I couldn't put my finger on it.

I pulled the chair out and was frustrated to see that it was broken, the seat completely caved in. I looked up at my grandma.

"Well, it's never going to work if you don't see it." She smiled.

I looked down again and concentrated on the feeling permeating the room. It was a feeling of warmth, safety, and *family*. I shook my head and when I looked at the chair, it wasn't broken anymore. The back was straight and the cherry wood was shining, reflecting the light from the chandelier. The black cushioned seat was embroidered with bright and happy flowers. I smiled to myself and sat down gingerly. Grant was on my left and he reached over to place a hand on my leg, smiling around a huge bite of food.

As soon as my rear end touched the chair, people were passing bowls to me, piling my plate high with food. I picked up a shiny silver spoon and ignoring the rasp of tarnish I felt as I held it, I shoved it under a fluffy pile of eggs. They steamed up into my face with a buttery, rich aroma. I placed the fork in my mouth and almost wept as the eggs melted in my mouth, filling me with warmth and energy. For the next few minutes, I didn't do anything but eat. I ate until the beast inside was sated and then I washed down my last bite with a cold glass of milk.

Grandma sat across from me, not eating, but regarding me over her folded hands. Her eyes twinkled and she smiled at me. "You ready to meet everyone now?"

I nodded and wiped at my face with a napkin that felt threadbare in my hands but appeared thick and luxurious. I took a look around the table at everyone talking and laughing with one another. There were eleven of us in all. Evie, Grant, Tristan, Andy, Grandma, the man next to me, three other men, a woman, and me.

My grandmother stood up, wiping at her mouth and then folding the napkin and placing it next to her plate. As she stood, the voices grew quiet and all eyes focused on her.

She cleared her throat. "As you know, this," she gestured across the table at me, "is Marissa."

Several people nodded and smiled at me. I sat back in my chair, uncomfortable being the center of attention at this bizarre dinner party. Grant reached over and placed his hand, palm up, on my leg. I put my hand in his and welcomed the strength I felt pouring from him to me when the connection was made.

"Sitting to your right is Martin Scott, host of tonight's festivities."

Martin smiled and held his hand out to me. His fingers were long and sinewy and his grip was strong.

He nodded at me and turned his attention back to my grandmother.

"Next to him is his son, Henry Scott, and his son, George."

Both men nodded at me, wide smiles on their faces. I tried to return the smile, but my mouth was too dry. I felt my tongue sticking to the roof of my mouth.

My grandma forged on. "This is Alice, George's daughter."

Alice stood and reached her hand across the table. "I am so pleased to make your acquaintance, Marissa. My great granddaughter has told us so much about you, and about how you tried to help our son. My Frederick and I will forever be indebted to you."

"Th-thank you," I murmured, pulling my hand back from her grasp. This was all getting to be too much and I felt like bolting from the table. Grant took my hand again and I pressed my fingers into his, holding tightly to what I felt was my last link to normalcy that I had. "I, um, I'm sorry, who is your son?"

She turned pretty brown eyes my way. "Why, Samuel, dear."

My hand flew to my mouth and my eyes filled with tears.

Alice's face fell. She turned to look at my grandma. "She did not know, Lydia?"

My grandmother shook her head. "I had hoped she wouldn't ever have reason to meet us all."

The light dimmed for a moment, and with it, the happy feeling. The tablecloth faded and fell apart in places, revealing the rotting wood of the table underneath. A ripping sound emanated from behind me as a sheet of brittle wallpaper tore itself from the wall.

My grandmother closed her eyes, took a deep breath, and the room returned to as it had been before. She sat down and looked across the table at me. "Marissa, Alice is Sam's mother, which means, you are sitting at the table with your entire family line."

"Wicked," Andy breathed. If I had been close enough, I would have kicked him under the table.

I looked around at the faces that resembled mine. There were my eyes and my nose. My hair and my smile. This was my family. I took a deep breath. "This is all a little much. I mean, wh-where did you all come from? Why haven't I met you all before? How are you all still here? How are you *here*? Why are you here? Are there others?" I paused, my chest heaving. "I'm not sure I understand."

Understatement of the year, Anderson.

I ignored him and stared across the table at my grandmother, waiting for an explanation.

"She deserves to know," Martin said. He was very soft-spoken, almost timid in his mannerisms as he lay the napkin next to his plate.

My grandmother peered at him. She raised her eyebrows and shook her head. "I'm not sure where to start."

Tristan placed a notebook on the table. He pointed with his pen at each person as he talked. "It goes Marissa Anderson, John Anderson, Lydia Anderson, Sarah Miller, Sam Johnson, Alice Johnson, George Scott, Henry Scott, and finally, Martin Scott. Did I miss anyone?"

Grandma smiled at him. She shook her head. "No, that's everyone back to, well, the early eighteen hundreds. Martin was the first of our family to settle in Culvers Grove."

Martin cleared his throat and glanced nervously out the window into the darkness.

"Why are you all here?" I asked, my voice small.

"The abbreviated answer to why we are all here," Henry said, "is that your grandmother gathered us and brought us to the only safe place in the town."

"A fact that you kids were smart enough to figure out as well," Grandma said with an affectionate glance my way.

I looked around. "You can all move around the town? You're not trapped where you, um, passed away?"

"Our movement can be limited by choice," Grandma said. "When I chose to stay with your grandfather, I was restricted to the kitchen in the house. Most of us chose to stay with our loved ones."

Her comment elicited nods around the table.

"But, they couldn't come here?"

"Most of them are already gone, child," Henry said. His eyes gleamed for a moment under the chandelier. "When Lydia came to get us, we had been awakened."

"Sam really did choose to stay at the courthouse?" Evie asked. Her voice was small.

"We don't know why Samuel chose to stay there," Alice said. "It was with a heavy heart that we said goodbye to him."

Evie sat back. "You were right, St. Louis."

Tristan glanced at Evie and then at me. He cleared his throat and then spoke. "So, Marissa's grandma brought you all here?"

Alice nodded. "She did."

"When Marissa told me that our family was being *collected,*" Grandma said, "I left that morning to get to our remaining family members before *it* did."

"I don't think it's after you all anymore," Evie said. She folded her napkin and sat back in the chair.

"We think that whatever it is wants me because I can help it get out." My statement was met with silence. "That's why it took my dad."

Grant squeezed my hand.

"Do you know what *it* is?" Tristan asked.

"We do not know. Only that something evil has been lying dormant underneath this town for many, many years." Alice paused, her dainty features creased with worry lines. "Somehow your appearance has awakened it and now it grows stronger with each passing day."

"How do we stop it?" I asked. No one offered an answer, but I let the question stretch out along the table. Several of them averted their eyes when I met theirs. "Really?" My voice was louder than I intended. "No one has anything to say? My dad, your *son*," I said pointedly at my grandmother, "is down there going on three days now. He's not going to last much longer, physically, but especially not mentally." I looked around the table again. When no one said anything, I stood up, throwing my napkin to the table. "Fine! You all sit around here reminiscing about the days of yore, or whatever. I'm going to get my dad." I started to stomp around the table, but I was stopped by the gentle touch of Martin.

He placed a warm hand on my arm. "You would not last but a minute. There are many dangerous things out there, and your signature on this world is strong. Stronger than any of us have ever seen."

"Signature?"

He nodded. "Yes, all of us have a unique imprint on the world around us."

"The weird color I can see around you," Evie said, "it's like a hole in the fabric."

"The fabric?" Alice asked.

I nodded. "Evie explained it once to me that there is a fabric of sorts between this world and the next. When ghosts are upset or trying to communicate, she can see a distortion in the fabric. She can also see colors around people, how they're feeling, you know, that sort of thing." My face grew hot as I realized everyone was staring at me. And I was still talking. "...but it's fading." I finished and sat down in my chair again.

"And how did she come to have these abilities?" George asked. His eyes sparkled in the light and a hint of a smile parted his lips.

I felt like he already knew the answer before I spoke. "Oh. Um, I let her soul pass through me when she was in a coma and she was dying."

The room was silent again.

"She was dying," I explained.

"Do any of your other friends have this ability?" he asked.

The jig is up, Anderson.

I tossed him a glare. *Should I tell them?*

The cat's out of the bag now, another voice interjected. *Might as well tell everyone.*

I looked over at my grandma and she winked at me.

"Um, so the smoke was trying to get into Andy and I pulled it out. I saw our lights meet for a minute in the middle and then I held onto the smoke until we passed through the barrier and got out of town."

Andy tapped the side of his head with a finger and winked. "I can talk to her, you know, with my mind now."

"He can also see the history of an object," I offered.

A rumble of voices spread through the room.

"What's going on?" I leaned over and whispered to Martin.

He regarded me with quiet eyes. "They want to see if he can see what history the object wrapped in your friend's coat in the credenza has to offer. In fact, I think I would like to do that now. Andrew?" Martin stood and placed his napkin on the table.

I shook my head. "I don't understand what the necklace has to do with anything," I said. "We need to be talking about how to get into the cave under the courthouse and rescue my dad."

Martin's gaze shifted slowly to me. "I believe the necklace is the key to doing just that, child."

My legs went numb and I was glad that I was seated on a chair. "The necklace is going to get my dad out of there?"

"It was something very important that was left in our care by Samuel. I, for one, would like to find out what was so special about it."

He left the room and came back, the coat bundled in his hands. I made a move to clear a spot on the table, but was surprised to see that the food had vanished. The white tablecloth spread out like a clean start in front of us.

Martin placed the coat on the table and then allowed the necklace to drop out onto the surface with a dull clunk.

We all sat quietly, taking in the tarnished piece of metal lying on the table. It was gold, or at least, it used to be and covered in an intricate flower, vining design. The shape of the bauble was oval, small and about the size of a rosebud. The chain wound around itself, creating the infinity sign on the table.

I felt Grant draw back at my side and reached over to take his hand. "It burned him," I said by way of explanation. True to form, I found myself babbling as I tried to explain the events of earlier. "Tristan and Grant went back to put chains on the truck and while they were there, they went out to the cemetery. Grant and I got chased out of there earlier by a huge crowd of ghosts that had black smoke around them. They made a portal and we almost fell through. I saw a, um, vision of grandma burying something near the gravestone of her baby and I was trying to get it because…well, because it seemed important…" I faded off, not sure anymore where my original line of thought had been pointing. My brain was tired and stressed, and I couldn't form anything resembling a coherent thought anymore.

Want to let me take it from here?

I nodded at Andy. *Yeah.*

"Tristan and Grant retrieved the object, this necklace, from the cemetery, but when they crossed out of the barrier, it began burning Grant." He smiled at me. *That wasn't so hard, was it?*

"We don't think it wanted to leave the town," I said.

"Do you remember where this came from, Lydia?" Alice asked.

Grandma shook her head. "I remember finding it on my nightstand one evening. It was there with a note scrawled in handwriting I didn't recognize."

"What did it say?" Tristan asked.

Grandma considered, lost in thought for a moment. "It said something about keeping it safe and how I was never to allow it to leave our bloodline."

"It was the same note that accompanied the necklace when you first gave it to me," Martin said.

She looked at him, her head tilted to the side. She stared at him through faded eyes. *Could it be?* "Mo-Mo?" Her withered hand flew to her mouth.

Andy leaned over to Evie. "Who's Mo-Mo?"

"The man from the forest," Evie said.

He shrugged.

"From the tape. Honestly," she said to Andy, "don't you pay attention to anything?"

Martin smiled at my grandmother. "We met when you were but a toddler. You were unable to pronounce my name, so I allowed you to call me Mo-Mo." He smiled again. "You were the only bright spot in a very lonely existence."

Grandma's eyes searched his. "You lived here, in the woods. Why didn't you tell me you were my family?"

Martin sat down and looked at my grandma. "Do you think it best to tell a small child that I was a ghost? A real thing? As it was, you could only claim me as a figment of your conjuring. You grew up, dismissed me as a childhood fancy."

"I am so sorry," she said. "I didn't know."

"How could you have?" he asked.

Grant cleared his throat. "Um, I hate to interrupt, but…"

I followed his gaze to the tabletop. The necklace stretched out on its chain, vibrating in the air.

I gulped. It was pointed right at me.

CHAPTER 26

Looks like it wants to dance, Anderson.

Get over here. I took a step back from the table and the necklace dropped innocuously onto the surface again. I stared at it.

Andy moved to stand beside me. *You got me if it goes haywire, right?*

I nodded.

He reached out his hand and grasped the oval. His arm went rigid.

"You okay?" I whispered.

He nodded. "Yeah. I see Grant and Tristan digging it up. There are ghosts all around as they run to the truck." He paused for a moment. "I see your grandma burying it in the cemetery. She's looking over her shoulder like she's hiding something."

"I didn't want anyone to see me. Everyone in town thought losing Isaiah sent me over the edge. I didn't want to fuel their fire." Her eyes were sad as they focused on the necklace.

"Now, I see it on a table. It's in a...a wooden shack. And you're there." He looked up at Martin. "You're staring at it."

"I was worried that she had forgotten to come back and get it."

"I guess I had," Grandma murmured.

"It's on a white vanity. In a jewelry box. Lots of sparkly stuff in there." Andy blinked several times. "I can see the reflection in the mirror. She looks like the woman in the picture Janice gave us."

"Sarah?" I asked.

"I think so."

"I remember now!" Grandma said. She shook her head. "How could I have forgotten all of this? I remember that my mother had the locket with the note. I was worried that Father would sell it when the Depression hit. He was selling anything that wasn't bolted down. So, I took it one day. I took it to you."

Martin nodded. "You left it with me and told me that you would be back for it."

"I never did, though. How did you get it to my nightstand?"

Martin smiled a bit. "That is one of my talents. As Marissa is able to see ghosts and converse with us in her mind, I am able to move things of the other world. That is," he looked down, "if I concentrate completely enough."

"It's in a box. A woman is pulling it out from under a plank under the bed. It's lonely. It hasn't seen the sun in so long. She is putting on a green dress and she's getting ready. Now, we're at a wedding. It's Sarah again. The woman is giving it to Sarah. Placing the box in among the flowers of her bouquet. She whispers that it is from her father."

"Sam," Evie mouthed.

"Now I'm seeing Sam. He's, um, doing something to the necklace. He's in a house and it's dark. He's, um…" Andy shut his eyes tight. "He's using a fire to, um, go around the edge of it and he's writing a note. Scrawling handwriting. 'My dearest Sarah. I love you with all my heart. Please keep this safe. Do not allow it to fall into the hands of anyone outside our bloodline.'" He shook his head. "Um, now he's at the courthouse. It's under construction, and um, it's nighttime. No one's there." Andy paused.

"I remember seeing that," I said. "When we were trying to find Sam, I saw that from the attic. He came in and went to the basement, but we couldn't get down there to see what he was doing."

"He's going down the stairs to the basement. There is a pile of rubble in the corner. He's approaching it, kicking it with his boot. There's so much sadness here, and um, scared. He's scared. He's trying to find something." Andy paused again, watching the scene play out behind his eyelids. "There it is. It's the necklace. It's lying there and it's open. It's a locket!" His eyes popped open and he looked down at the object in his hand. "It's a locket. Why did he weld it closed?" Before we could begin to speculate, Andy threw his head back. "It's open and it's watching him. There's a woman's face. He's scared, but he picks it up with the stick. It's dangling, turning around and around while it's hanging there."

I reached out while Andy was talking and touched his arm. White heat passed through my fingertips and I was able to see what he was seeing.

I started talking. "Sam took it. He held it in his hand and it didn't hurt him. The smoke is coming out, staring at him, but it can't take him. It's, um, repelled. It's trying to pull him in, trying to get at his soul, but it can't."

Andy stopped for a second and looked at me. *You can see this, Anderson?*

I nodded. "Go on."

Andy took a deep breath and then concentrated on the locket again. "It's daytime now. Sam is working in the basement with another man. He's in the corner, breaking up rock with a pickaxe. Sam looks up when the man cries out. He walks over and watches the man bend over to pick something up from the ground. He stands up and holds out his hand. It's, it's the locket. The man smiles and says he's going to give it to his wife. Now, he's opening it…and…oh my God." Andy stopped and dropped the locket to the table. He took a step back from it, breaking our connection in the process.

"What did you see?" Grandma asked.

"As soon as the man opened the locket, I could see something beyond it. A, a cavern of some sort. There was a bright light on one side and a darkness on the other. Then, black smoke shot out from it and the wall collapsed. The man was buried underneath the rubble. Sam tried to save him, but it was too late."

Tristan had his phone out. "His name was Carter Jefferson. I remember looking him up when we were looking for Sam."

"I remember that, too." I swallowed. The image of the terror in the man's face became seared into my memory. "Andy, I need you to look at the locket again."

Not a chance.

You're scared?

You bet your butt, I am.

I pressed my lips together. *Come on, I can't do it myself.*

He glowered at me for a moment. "Fine, but you owe me, like, twelve pizzas."

I didn't miss the tremor in his voice. Nodding, I reached out for his arm again as he approached the table and picked up the locket.

Suddenly, there were more. A man in a cowboy hat, riding a horse, picking up the locket from the ground. He smiled as he opened it and then the black smoke came up, winding around his arms, as he stood frozen to the spot. He cried out as an arrow sizzled through the air, piercing his heart. A flash of a woman, her hand around the locket, peering down at the woman's face contained within as the smoke caressed her face. She was beautiful, young, and then, she was crying out in pain. She looked down at her feet in confusion at the tangle of rattlesnakes boiling around her ankles, drawing back and striking over and over again. A flash of another man in a suit, his life ending as a fire overtook him on the prairie. He died with the locket grasped in his palm, the black smoke intermingling with the smoke from the fire. Another flash, and another, all people dying in agony. My heart ached for them as I related each terrible story to the people around the table. A flash and I saw a Native American walking up to a barren circle of earth. It was the same man I'd seen in the clearing the day before. I watched him die, eaten up by the ground itself. His last moments on earth full of misery.

Tears ran down my face. A final flash. "Now, it's dark. There's a fire and a man. He's alone. His horse is tied nearby. He's staring down at the locket. He's crying. Coughing. Oh, it sounds horrible." I peered closer at the vision. The heat from the fire rose in waves, distorting what I thought I saw.

Andy, can you get closer?

Andy nodded, his mouth drawn tight in concentration.

The vision shifted as Andy drew closer. The man was so sad. So sick.

Go around the fire. I have to see something.

Andy moved closer and to the side.

Now the vision was clear. The man stared down at the locket he held in one hand and a letter he held in the other, his eyes wavering among the tears. His mouth was drawn back in a cry of complete and utter hopelessness. As I watched, the smoke came out of not only the locket, but the man as well. It rose like a column of darkness, meeting above his head with the black smoke that already resided there. It spun around in the air, and then jettisoned back into him, pouring an inky viscous substance into him that splattered on his face. He coughed again, the smoke coming out of him, circling around him, claiming him. It spun around him, in him, tightening its black cords of evil. His head shot back and he gazed up at the stars with hollow eyes.

One last cry escaped his lips and he choked on the overwhelming blackness, his last breaths a horrible gurgling sound. He stopped breathing, the locket falling to the ground as he died. The smoke overtook him, circling around until it was all I could see. With a sonic boom that extinguished the fire, the column of smoke shot down through the open locket.

Get closer, I urged, squeezing Andy's arm.

Are you crazy? Did you not just see what happened?

Get closer. It's a memory. It can't hurt you.

Andy shook his head once and then closed his eyes again. He moved closer.

I looked down and saw the letter floating to the ground. It was lit by moonlight and the beautiful looping script stood out in dark contrast to the paper. I squinted as I read.

Dearest Jacob,

Your absence these past months has left me longing for your smile, your touch, your love. Mattie misses you as well, though she has not yet met you. Please come back to us soon, my love. No one shall ever possess my heart as you do.

Devotedly, your Charlotte

The darkness closed in again and I looked up. I saw the black smoke passing into the locket. But, as I tilted my head, I realized it wasn't actually passing into the locket, but *through* it. The smoke disappeared and the woman's face was left, staring up at me with a bemused look on her face. Her hair was swept up into a loose bun on the top of her head and she wore a high-necked white shirt. She was severe, but almost pretty. I leaned closer, wanting to see more. The memory was beginning to fade around the edges already. I reached out to touch the locket.

Suddenly, the woman's head moved. She looked up at me and smiled.

You're next, she mouthed.

CHAPTER 27

My eyes fluttered open and I stared up at the crumbling ceiling of Sarah's house. I was in the living room, lying on the threadbare couch that was little more than a rotting frame and stuffing that turned to dust with any touch. It was dark and I was alone. I sat up quickly, immediately reaching up to touch my head. There was a bandage on my forehead and I winced as I touched it.

"You're awake." My grandma stood in the doorway, a lantern held up in her hand. She looked around the room. "This will never do," she murmured. The room shifted, the former splendor returning to the walls, the floor, and the objects in the space. A fire appeared in the fireplace, roaring with a warmth that filled me with energy.

Grandma walked over and touched my head. "You passed out in the dining room. Fell and hit your head on the table." She smiled. "'Bout as graceful as I used to be."

I sat up and took a drink of water from the glass she placed on the coffee table. It was clear and cold.

"I have to tell you what happened in the vision," I said, starting to stand.

Grandma placed a hand on my shoulder. "Your friend, Andy, filled us in. It seems the locket has been taking souls now for a very long time."

"If we open it, do you think it would continue to do that?"

She nodded thoughtfully. "I believe so. That is why Sam thought it so important to keep it in our family. Had it fallen into other hands and they would have attempted to open it…" her voice faded and she shuddered. "As it is, it has been kept safe and unable to carry out its purpose since your great-great-grandfather's time."

"You think it was *made* to take souls?" A shiver ran through me.

She stared at me. "Yes, I think it is an object of evil."

"Why didn't anyone try to destroy it?"

"Well, until your friend saw its history, none of us knew it *should* be destroyed. Now, however, it seems it will be impossible."

I tilted my head and looked at her.

"Come with me." She held out her hand to me.

I took it, amazed at the energy that filled me when I did so. I followed her through the dining room and butler's pantry to the kitchen beyond. Through the back window, I could see my family and friends gathered around in the moonlight.

"What are they doing?"

She sighed. "Trying to destroy it. They've been at it for over an hour now and nothing seems to mar it."

I watched for another moment through the window then walked outside, the cold air biting at me through my shirt.

Tristan had his phone out. "Fire doesn't work. We've tried a hammer, water, driving over it with Andy's truck. Now, we've tried burying it. By the way," he turned to Andy, "your parents say that they're fine and that we should stay in Kirksville for another night."

"We're in Kirksville?" I cocked my eyebrow.

Tristan smiled. "I don't know where you and Evie are, but Andy and I are up in Kirksville visiting Truman's campus. My dad doesn't approve, but he decided to allow it so I could get it out of my system before they send me off to Stanford." He rolled his eyes.

"How are your parents?" I looked at Grant.

He came over to me and kissed the top of my head. His eyes focused on my forehead and he brushed my hair back in a gentle motion. "They're fine. They think I'm back in KC getting some studying done while the dorms are quiet. How are you?"

"I'm fine." I shrugged. "I mean, considering."

He nodded and took off his coat, draping it around my shoulders.

"What do we do now?" I asked, my breath hanging in a cloud.

Everyone was quiet and I realized they were all staring at the ground. The locket had dug itself out and was floating in the air, tethered to the ground by the chain. It was pointed straight at me. I took a step to the side and it mimicked my movement.

"Why is it doing that?" I asked, my voice shaky.

"We don't know. It seems to be pulled to you." Henry stood leaning on a shovel. "It won't stay underground with you around."

"Keeps popping back up," Andy said.

I squinted at him. His eyes looked worried.

You okay?

Yeah, wishing I could un-see some of the stuff I saw tonight.

I nodded and took a step closer to the locket. It practically vibrated on the chain.

Grant pulled me back. "I don't think that's a good idea."

I turned to him and handed him his coat. "It can't hurt anyone while it's closed."

He took the coat and folded it over his arm. "Be careful."

"I promise." I approached the locket and bent over, wrapping my fingers carefully around it. The ground released its hold and the chain hung limply from my hand. I felt something dark emanating from the object in my palm. *Marissssa.* It was subdued, but it was angry. I shook my head and pushed the feeling away. As suddenly as it came, the feeling was gone and the object was quiet.

I looked around to see if anyone had heard anything. Everyone's faces were blank, though. Andy peered at me, but didn't say anything, either out loud or in my head. I took a calming breath and placed the chain around my neck.

Grant started to protest, but my grandma placed a hand on his arm. "It's okay, Grant. She's fine."

I swallowed, waiting to see if anything would happen or if I would hear anything again. There was only silence. I was surprised to find that the locket felt at home hanging around my neck. I looked up at Grant. "It feels right. Is that weird?"

He smiled. "We're in a house with your entire ghost family in a town taken over by a black smoke monster, and you think *this* might be the thing that qualifies as weird?"

I shook my head. "So, how are we going to stop this thing under the courthouse and get my dad back?"

"Sam, too," Evie said.

"And Sarah," I finished. Here, bolstered by the spirits of my family, I felt, for the first time in days, that everything was going to turn out all right.

Pretty ambitious, Anderson.

I shot him a smile and walked back into the house. "Tristan, can you bring the maps and your phone projector?"

Everyone followed me inside where I placed the map of the cave system on the dining room table. Grandma walked in and started to light everything up.

"Leave it dark, please. Tristan?"

He switched out his phone case and held up the projector, overlaying the map of the town onto the cave. I grabbed a pen from Tristan's backpack and started circling entrances. "Henry, here. George, here. Grandma, Alice, and Martin, here, here, and here. Evie and Andy, here." I placed a red circle on the quarry. "Tristan and Grant will come with me here." I drew an arrow in through the speakeasy to the courthouse.

Grant's brow furrowed. "Why us?"

"Because we aren't part of the club. Remember?" Tristan replied.

I nodded. "We talked about this before. We have more ammunition now, more spirits that can pull the BB's attention in more ways."

"That's gonna' be a hard no, Anderson. We all need to go in together."

"Sure, we'll be a great big beacon. You and Evie have part of me with you. It'll be enough to pull the attention on its own."

"St. Louis's right. It's the only way to get her in there. We can circle around after we pull the ghost squad's attention and follow them in." She looked up at me. "I think it will work."

"Won't they hone in on your signal?" Grant asked me.

"Not if we are stronger," George said. His mouth was set in the way Dad's was when he had a project.

I smiled, and then felt tears prick at the back of my eyes. *Dad.*

"We'll light up that cave like Christmas Eve," Grandma said.

"I don't think you should do this," Grant said.

I looked over at him.

"That's cute," Andy said. "He thinks he has a say in Miss Independent's plan."

I mentally flipped him off.

Andy shook his head. "He's right, though. This is crazy. Even if you do manage to get in to your dad, how are you going to get him out?"

"We'll make a portal." I looked around at my family. "*We* can create one like the ghosts in the cemetery did. We'll meet under the courthouse and make one together."

Everyone stared at me.

"Only ghosts can travel through the portals," Tristan said.

"The portal was pulling at my *body*. A few more minutes and we both would have been pulled in."

"Fine, so we create a portal and get all of us and your dad out. What about your family?"

I looked around at them.

My grandma reached out to take my hand. Hers were soft and warm. She licked her lips, her eyes unwavering. "Marissa, we're already dead. You're not. Your dad is alive. Getting you all out is what's important here."

I felt the tears dangerously close to the surface and shook my head. "No, we can get everyone out. We have to."

She smiled sadly. "We'll see how it goes. Lord knows I hope that it goes well and we get everyone out, but if things go all cattywampus down there, you focus on getting you, your dad, and your friends out. You understand me?"

It wasn't a question.

I swallowed and looked at my relatives. Each one in turn nodded their heads, giving me their blessing and their strength. I drew in a deep breath and nodded my head. "Everyone ready?"

"Yeah, St. Louis, we're ready."

CHAPTER 28

Andy drove along the back roads of the country with his foot mashed to the accelerator. We'd all left the sanctuary of Sarah's home at midnight after fueling up on food, medicine, and energy from my family. When we left the triangle, there was a heaviness, but no one was affected as they had been before. We'd bought ourselves some time. The tension in the truck was palpable. No one spoke as we followed the bright ribbon of gravel road through the moonlit night.

Each turn we made had us holding our breath, certain we would see a barrier of ghosts and smoke barring the way. All seemed quiet, though, and we made it to the location of the speakeasy without incident. Grant, Tristan, and I got out of the truck and stood staring at Andy's brake lights as he and Evie headed back to the quarry. After they left, the silence closed in on us, its own physical presence in the night.

Tristan pointed with his flashlight. "Through here."

Grant and I followed him through the thick underbrush and snow on the side of the road. We made our way through about half a mile of tangled terrain until we reached the edge of a grove of trees. An old barn stood sentry in front of a cliff wall rising up into the night. Tristan used his light to examine the rock face.

"There," he breathed. His light was trained on a large opening to the side of the barn. Almost completely hidden in a tangle of brush and trees, it was about the loneliest place I'd ever seen.

"You ready?" Grant asked.

I nodded and reached up to hold the locket. It vibrated in my grasp, reaching out toward the cave opening. "Let's go."

We had decided I would not do anything to draw attention to myself, including using my abilities to see any visions. Grant took my arm and guided me through the snow to the cave opening.

Once we got closer, we could see that the opening rose about seven feet into the hillside and was over six feet wide. We ducked through the opening and stood in a large cavern. There were the remnants of the speakeasy. A wooden bar and tables had succumbed to the constant moisture of the cave and lay in rotting piles on the wide expanse of flat floor. A space near the edge rose a bit above the rest and it would have been the perfect place for a stage. I heard the phantasmal strumming of a bass and the lilting melody of a horn echoed above me. I gritted my teeth and shut down the vision from the past before it had a chance to solidify.

Grant helped me out of my coat. He folded it and placed it on the floor of the cavern. "You okay?" he asked.

I nodded. "I'm fine."

"Over here," Tristan said. He was standing near the back wall, his light illuminating a small tunnel leading off into the darkness. "The map shows it's about a mile hike to the courthouse from here. Looks like a straight shot for the most part."

"For the most part?" Grant hissed as he followed us into the tunnel.

"There's one fork up ahead. We have to take it to the left."

"What's on the right?"

"The quarry."

"Won't the ghosts have to pass through there?" *To get to Andy and Evie,* I finished in my head.

"Yeah, but by the time we get there, they'll be long gone. The fork is really close to the courthouse. It'll be fine."

We made our way along the tunnel, shuffling our feet as Tristan led the way, his light sweeping the darkness in front of him. Stopping occasionally to listen for any sign of company, the only sound we heard was the dripping of water along the walls.

We had covered some distance when Tristan stopped short. He shone his flashlight at a wall in front of us. "This isn't supposed to be here. It's not on the map. The fork isn't until we get further in."

"Which way do we go?" Grant asked.

I stared at the three openings in front of us. Tristan turned to look at me. "I'm sorry, Marissa. It's not on the map."

I took a deep breath. "We'll figure it out. You said we had to choose the left at the fork, we'll choose the left here, too. That'll work, right?"

He didn't look convinced. "This area is closest to the river and it's the oldest. There are tunnels leading all over this area. Some of them double back, turn into dead ends, and end in tunnels so tangled that we'd never be able to find our way out."

My insides dropped. "We have to figure out a way," I said, my voice plaintive in the darkness. "We can't turn back now."

"I don't know what to do here, Marissa."

"Can we use our reflective tape?" Grant asked.

"We can, but I don't know how long we'd be lost down here." Tristan sounded defeated. "Let me think." He pulled up his phone and stared at the picture he'd taken of the cave map. He used his fingers to pinch and make certain parts larger, poring over the screen, his gaze intense. Suddenly, he looked up and flicked off his phone and the flashlight.

"What's wrong?" I asked.

"Shhhh. Do you hear that?"

I stood perfectly still, not even breathing as I listened for any sound at all. "I don't think…" My voice caught in my throat as I heard it. A shuffling sound coming down the tunnel. My heart thundered loudly in my chest. I listened again. *That's not right. It's coming from behind us.* With that realization, I plastered myself against the wall, my teeth chattering.

The noise grew louder, shuffling footsteps now, coming our way from behind us. The fear was coursing through me, making my middle cramp as my muscles filled with adrenaline. I closed my eyes and started to reach out, to see if I could tell what was coming our way. I tensed as I did and Grant grabbed my hand.

"Don't," he whispered. "You'll call them to us."

The footsteps halted for a moment, then headed toward us again. I couldn't move, couldn't think, couldn't feel. Then, I got mad. I at least wanted to look it in the eye before it took me. I grabbed at Tristan's hand, yanking the flashlight from it. I flipped it on, flooding the tunnel with light. It took a moment for my eyes to adjust, but when they did, I cried out and almost dropped the flashlight.

"Hey, what are y'all doin' down here?" A huge man in a black and white striped uniform stood in front of us. He had a shaggy beard and blue eyes. A smile lit up his features. "Did you find a way out?"

Chapter 29

I stared at the man in the tunnel. "Um, I'm Marissa and these are my friends, Grant and Tristan. Who are you?"

He shuffled forward and I saw that his ankles were shackled. "I'm Trent Sampson. Have you seen my partner? He's always gettin' lost down here."

"The bank robbers that escaped back in the thirties," Tristan whispered. "There were two of them and they died down here in the caves."

"Then why didn't their spirits leave? They weren't from Culvers Grove."

Tristan shrugged. "Maybe their spirits couldn't find their way out of the caves either?"

I swallowed, letting the sadness of his statement settle in on me. I turned. "I'm sorry; we haven't seen your partner. We're trying to get to the courthouse from here. Do you know how to get there?"

He smiled again. "Of course, but wild horses couldn't drag me back there! I'm looking for my partner and then we've got to get on home to Texas. You all seen him?"

I shook my head again. "No, sir. Could you at least show us which opening leads to the courthouse?"

He regarded us for a moment. "You want to tell me why I'd do that?"

"Because we know how to get out of here," Tristan said.

The man squinted, his eyes small and pig-like. "The one on the left."

"He's lying," I said.

The man regarded us for another moment. I felt the sadness coming from him swell in the tunnel, pushing me back into the wall.

"It gets awful lonely down here. Would sure be nice to have people to talk to." Trent's eyes glinted.

I cleared my throat. "My friend has a map of the caves. If you help us, he'll leave it for you. You can find your partner and get out."

Trent stood, his mouth working as he sized us up. "Promise?" he asked.

"We promise. Help us get to the fork and we'll leave the map for you," Tristan said.

Trent nodded his head once and then brushed past us, the cold, rotting scent of despair that rose up from him filling my nostrils. Tristan turned on his flashlight and Grant and I followed him through the open space. Grant stopped to place a huge arrow of reflective tape on both sides of the middle tunnel. The floor began to slope downward here, and my shoes had trouble finding traction on the slippery surface. It was much narrower than the previous tunnel and the walls closed in on my shoulders as I walked. I could hear Grant breathing hard behind me as he made his way along the dark passage.

Up ahead, Tristan's flashlight beam finally spilled out into a large cavern. We stepped into the space and I took the opportunity to stretch my arms above my head.

"There's the fork," Tristan said with a smile. "We're back on the grid."

I turned to the man. "Thank you, Trent. We appreciate the help."

He watched with hungry eyes as Tristan retrieved the map from his backpack and spread it out on the cavern floor with reverence.

I patted Tristan's arm when he stood up. "You can get another copy from Janice."

"Yeah, I know. He needs it more than I do." Tristan pulled a small camping lantern from the backpack and placed it on the floor next to the map. He turned it on, lighting up the entire place with a ghostly blue-white light.

Trent stared at the map for several minutes. Then, he looked up at us. "Have you seen my partner? I'd sure like to show him this."

I shook my head. "I'm sorry. We haven't seen him, but if we do, we'll tell him you're looking for him."

Trent tilted his head. With the shaggy beard clinging to his face, he reminded me of a cocker spaniel. "Y'all hear that? Darn things are back. They've been movin' around a lot lately."

I listened and felt the familiar grip of fear as the sound of several ghosts moving along the corridors reached my ears.

"Evie and Andy must have made it to the quarry later than we expected," Grant whispered.

I nodded, then reached over and squeezed his hand. My teeth gritted together. The sound of the spirits approaching filled my senses and I drew back, pressing myself against the wall again. My mind spun, thinking of and then rejecting options in a frustrating cycle. We could go back the way we came, but we would only end up having the ghosts follow us out, and we have no way to make it back to Sarah's. We could try to hide, but there was nowhere for us to do that. Hot tears filled my eyes as the sloshy sounds got louder and closer.

A moment later, they appeared in the opening, the black smoke urging them along the tunnels. My heart beat against my ribcage.

"You all aren't gettin' my map!" Trent shouted suddenly, his voice filling the chamber and startling me from my indecision. "You hear me? Y'all just move along!" He stood protectively over the map, waving his arms and shouting.

The horde of spirits moved past him, funneling into the next tunnel toward the quarry. A couple of them looked in our direction, but they were soon preoccupied with the giant man in stripes lobbing wild punches at their heads. They passed by him as he swung and spit and hollered. He made so much noise I clapped my hands over my ears. Tristan and Grant did the same.

Finally, the group passed and Trent stopped yelling. I let my hands drop from my ears and stood perfectly still, listening as the sounds of the horde moving further away down the tunnel faded. I let out the breath I had been holding and turned to see Grant. His face was unreadable. I almost asked him if he had had enough, but then he focused on me, his eyes softening in the lantern light. He pulled me against him and kissed the top of my head.

Tristan ventured over to the fork and listened. "I think it's safe now," he said, shining his light into the abyss on the left.

Trent lowered his enormous frame onto the floor and sat staring at the map. He looked up as Grant and I passed. "Y'all seen my partner?"

"Goodbye. I hope you find your way out," I said as I followed Tristan into the tunnel.

Grant held my hand as we made our way toward the middle of town. Toward the courthouse basement.

Toward my dad.

CHAPTER 30

Tristan, Grant, and I stood, staring down into the well in the basement of the courthouse. Nothing moved. Everything around us was eerily quiet as Tristan set up the pulley system to lower us down. We didn't speak as we went about the process.

When it was all set up and lit by lanterns, Tristan looked at me. "Everything's set. I made it so we can each lower ourselves down."

I nodded, understanding that we couldn't leave anyone alone up here.

"We have to wait for Evie and Andy," he said.

Grant cast a wary eye at the well. "Is that safe? Why isn't anything trying to stop us?"

I licked my lips and leaned against his side. "Because it wants me here."

I felt him shudder next to me as he wrapped an arm around my shoulders and pulled me close. "I don't want to lose you," he murmured into my hair.

I heard a noise behind me. A light flashed and Andy emerged from the hole in the back of one of the cells. Evie came through next.

"They're not far behind us," he panted as he stood up and brushed dirt from his knees.

Tristan walked over and wrapped Andy in a hug. "You're all right?"

Andy nodded and hugged him. "We're fine. It took us a little longer to get into the quarry. Someone had put up a temporary gate, so we had to knock out the cameras and ram it down. Lucille's a little beat up, but we're fine."

Tristan drew in a deep breath and hugged Andy again.

Evie stood near the well, her hand rubbing her arm. She stared down at the opening.

I walked over and stood next to her. "You going to be okay going down there again?"

She looked up at me with wide eyes. "Sam's down there?"

I peered over the edge. "And our dad."

Evie sniffed loudly. "Our dad," she repeated, her voice soft.

"Listen, I hate to be the bearer of bad news, but we've got about three minutes before the ghost crew shows up and sucks out our souls. You ready, Anderson?"

I turned to look at my friends. Tears sprang to my eyes. "I don't deserve any of you. You guys are the best friends I've ever had and I love you."

"That sounds dangerously like you're saying goodbye," Grant said. He came over and kissed me. His lips were soft and he smelled like summer days and walks in the woods and safety. I melted.

He drew back. "Everything is going to be fine. You have to believe that."

Because we all do.

I looked at Andy and nodded my head once. I took a deep breath. "Let's get down there."

I settled into the harness and dropped my legs over the side.

"When you get down there, don't do anything until we get down, too. Understand?" Evie brushed her curls back from her face.

"Not a thing."

"Should she really be going *first*?" she asked the group.

"If any of us go alone, it'll take us. She's got the best chance."

I felt the rope slide and I was making the descent. I held a flashlight in my mouth as I twisted, spiraling down into the cavern below. Like I had the first time I'd been here, I twisted in open space before my feet hit solid ground. I was pointed away from the cavern and crouched to the ground, yanking off the harness before sending it back up again.

I spun around, flattening myself against the wall of the cave. In front of me was Sam's body, twisted on the floor. I looked past that and saw the man in the light. The darkness pressed in from the other side. This time, something was different, though. The sphere of light surrounding the man was much smaller, and the darkness was almost all encompassing. I moved along the wall, toward the scene for a better look.

Evie alit behind me and the buckles on the harness tinkled as she took it off and sent it back up the well again. She came up next to me and crouched down.

"Does it know we're here?"

I nodded.

"Then, why isn't it doing anything?"

"It doesn't have to. I came to it. Come on." I moved along the wall again and now my view was completely unobscured. I began to make out shapes in the darkness. Spirits cried out, pressing against the smoky blackness with wails of despair. It brought tears to my eyes and I swiped at them with my sleeve. "It's bigger than last time we were here."

Holy crap, Anderson. This is nuts!

I turned to look at Andy. He was unfolding his lanky frame from the harness.

"St. Louis!" Evie hissed.

I spun around and followed Evie's line of vision. I cried out and my knees buckled.

There, sitting against a wall, his knees drawn up to his chest, was my dad. His glasses were askew and he sat staring blankly into the space around him. Black smoke circled his wrists and ankles, binding him to the floor. I made a move to run down there, but Andy grabbed my arm.

Wait for the others.

A sob wrenched itself from my core. *It's my dad.*

I know. I know.

Tristan appeared next and we waited. I watched the bottom of the well for what seemed like hours before Grant's feet and then his legs appeared. He climbed out of the harness and came over.

"What took you so long?"

He jerked his head behind him. "They showed up."

I watched as my family emerged from the well. Martin, Henry, George, Alice, and my grandma planted their feet firmly on the ground and walked over.

My chin quivered and my voice caught in my throat. "He's there," I pointed.

Grandma pulled me to her and gave me a hug. Energy flowed. "We love you, Marissa. All of us. Don't you ever feel alone." She squeezed one last time and then turned to the others. "You all know what to do?"

They nodded and we walked down the slope toward the darkness. Together.

CHAPTER 31

You didn't think it would be easy, did you, Anderson?

Well, I didn't really know what to expect.

The moment we took our first step and began our descent is when everything started going wrong. Ghosts began to pour from the well behind us, as if someone above had turned on a faucet. They fell one on top of the other, the sound of their bodies slamming into each other turning my stomach. *They don't have bodies,* I told myself. The sound begged to differ, though. It was like dropping wet rags on a concrete floor and I felt bile rising in my throat. The spirits rose from the pile, their hollow eyes focused as they moved with jerky movements toward us.

We were focused on the approaching horde when I heard someone cry out. I spun around. The black smoke pulled George from the group. My grandma made a wild grab at his feet as he passed by overhead, but she only managed to brush her fingertips against the sole of his shoe. The smoke pulled him into the darkness. He writhed, screaming in agony as he disappeared.

"Huddle up," Grandma ordered and my family circled around us. "Keep moving."

We worked our way toward my dad. The ghosts kept up their relentless pursuit behind us and the darkness sent out tendrils of smoke to our group, dancing around the periphery, waiting for its chance to snatch one.

My vision was tunneled as I stared at my dad, willing him to look at me, to be okay.

Marissssa. I froze, almost tripping Andy who was right next to me.

Watch it.

Did you hear that?

He cocked his head to the side. *I didn't hear anything.*

You two be quiet. And pay attention! My grandmother's voice was stern.

I looked up as we got nearer to the darkness. Hans' image floated in front of me, pressed against the smoky barrier. He was burning and crying out, the skin on his face blistering like it had been when Evie broke the doll. I slammed my eyelids shut and turned my head away.

I opened them when I heard another voice cry out. Black smoke circled Henry's neck, pulling him back toward the darkness. I cried out and grabbed his hands, holding on for all I was worth. A final yank and he was pulled from my grasp, his strangled cries filling the cavern.

"We have to go back!" Tristan yelled.

"We can't," Andy said. "There's no other way out."

"They can make a portal! Make a portal and get us out of here! We can come back for him later!" The fear had made Tristan's voice raspy and foreign. His eyes rolled wildly in his head and he was almost past the point of being rational.

I grabbed his hand. "Tristan, we are going to be okay. We are going to get to my dad and we will get out. Stay with us."

He nodded and clamped his mouth down.

I turned my attention back to my dad. We were only about ten feet from him. "I'm going to pull the smoke off him and you guys make the portal?" I whispered.

That's the plan, my dear.

I nodded and prepared my body for the fight. Nine feet. Eight. Seven.

At two feet, I broke from the group and slid on my knees to my dad's side. Tears streamed down my face as I pulled at the black smoke. It stretched like taffy, but it wouldn't release its hold. I focused on pulling it from him to me. As I pulled, Dad turned to look at me.

Dark circles ringed his eyes and he looked exhausted, and sad.

"Hey, Peanut."

Something inside me broke and I lost it. My concentration wavered and I looked up to see Alice battling against the smoke that had wrapped itself around her midsection.

It has to be now, Marissa. Our circle's getting awful small.

I focused all of my attention on the black smoke circling my dad's wrists. The shadow of Alice's spirit passed over me as she was pulled into the darkness, but I didn't look up. I didn't look at anything except my dad. I pulled, allowing it to stretch from him to me. I welcomed the searing pain as it wrapped around my middle. I gritted my teeth against a scream as the smoke tried to burrow into my skin. With a mighty growl, I grabbed hold of it and cast it aside, ripping a layer of skin from my stomach in the process. Grant helped me pull my dad from the ground.

Grandma and Martin made a circle with their arms around him and closed their eyes. A portal opened up, the vortex tossing my hair around my face. Sarah's house was on the other side, the living room lit up by a solitary lantern.

I stared at the space between Grandma and Martin's arms. *It won't fit all of us!*

You didn't think it was going to be easy, did you, Anderson?

Well, I didn't know what to expect.

Send them. I'll stay with you.

They won't go.

He winked. *Yeah, they will.*

My eyes filled with tears and I nodded at Andy.

"Get her dad out of town!" Andy shouted as we shoved Tristan, Evie, and Grant into the circle with my dad.

I watched as they spun around and around. For a sickening moment, I didn't think it would work. They seemed to spin in place for an eternity. Then, a huge explosion as the portal disappeared. It threw all of us to the ground. We scrambled to our feet and circled up.

"Can you do it again?" I asked my grandma. When she didn't answer, I repeated myself. "Do you think you can make another portal?"

I stared at my grandma's face. Her mouth was drawn back in a smile. I looked closer. No, not a smile. A grimace. Of pain. I stared at her, not understanding. Then I saw it. The black smoke crept along the side of her neck, and then more tendrils, dripping from her scalp onto her face, obscuring her features.

"Grandma!" I shouted, lunging forward.

I love you, Marissa. Tell my son I love him, too. Let him know I've always been proud to be his mama.

"No!" I cried, flailing my arms after her as she was ripped from our group, her face covered in the hateful blackness. A moment later, she disappeared into the darkness. I fell to the ground, everything in my body and soul crying out in agony. The sound of anguish that rose from me was foreign to my ears, but all too familiar to my heart.

Something inside me shifted and felt like a plug had been pulled. The emotion poured through me, trying to fill up the hole, but it was draining faster than I could fill it up. I felt a hand on my shoulder and I looked up into my friend's face. Sobs wracked my body as he pulled me to my feet and held me against him. Martin wrapped us in his arms protectively, shielding us from the approaching horde from behind.

I'm sorry, Anderson.

I'm sorry, too. It wasn't supposed to turn out like this.

I know.

I took a deep breath and stood there, watching the black smoke approaching. It snaked along the ground, intent on us as it moved, slithering with calculated movements as it came to claim what belonged to it. I felt a tug on my neck and looked to see the locket had worked its way out from my collar and it was pulled straight out from my body. Pulling me forward. Toward the darkness.

Chapter 32

The locket tugged on me again. It was insistent, unrelenting. My neck burned where the chain cut into it on the back. It felt like the only thing holding me together. Keeping my pieces from scattering on the rock floor.

I took a step forward.

Um, whatcha' doin', Anderson?

It wants me to go to the darkness.

Yeah, I'm not gonna' let you do that.

You can't stop me.

Martin can get you to safety, but he can't take both of us.

Stop it!

Hands shoved me to the side and I fell back into Martin's arms. He held onto me, his eyes closed as he concentrated on creating a portal.

"Don't watch," he said, his voice strangled.

I ripped away from Martin's grasp and ran toward my friend.

Not this time!

Andy sprinted down the slope, toward the darkness. "Hey, BB! Show me what you've got!"

He charged directly into the darkness as Sam had done when he was saving Evie. And like when Sam had sacrificed himself to the darkness, once again, I felt arms close around me, bathing me in light and shielding me from the dark's grasp, as I watched my friend disappear in the cloud.

"No!" I shouted, my throat ripped raw. "Andy!"

Ugísa^n. A whisper in my ear. A voice filled with the exhaustion of an almost two-century long battle.

I turned to see the man in the light. Martin and I were bathed in the warm glow. Safe. I blinked several times, trying to see the features of the man.

"Who are you?" I wondered aloud.

I am MingkéHá.

The figure solidified and I saw the Native American from the grove in the field. His face was serene, but the muscles in his body were taut and he was breathing hard.

"I met you," I said, my speech slurring. I shook my head to clear it. "You were the one in the grove. I saw you die. I saw the locket pull you under the ground."

When I died, I was given a choice. I could leave and be with the spirits of my family or I could stay here and hold the curse at bay. I chose to stay here and keep everyone I loved safe from its influence.

"But, your people left years ago. Why are you still here?"

The people of this town, this earth, are all my people. He took a deep breath, the sphere of light flickering as he did so. *Ugísa^n.*

"Ugísa^n. You need my help?"

He nodded. *We all do. It grows stronger with each passing hour.*

I shook my head. "I don't know how to help."

Yes, you do.

Then, I knew. I knew what I had to do. I had to trap the darkness back inside the locket from where it came. I had to trap it in there and then become its guardian. I had to choose to keep my friends, my family, the town, and my people safe.

I turned to Martin. "I'm scared."

He regarded me with kind eyes. "I'll be with you the whole way, Marissa. You will not be alone."

The locket pulled on my neck again and I took a deep breath. "We have to get it open."

I held it in my hands and then MingkéHá's hands were around it, too. They trembled, creating a white-hot fire that didn't burn. He guided my fingers around the edges of the locket. The metal glowed red as my finger cut into it. He released my hands and I held the locket in my palms, cupped between my hands.

The cries of the spirits in the darkness broke into our cocoon of light, pressing down on the bubble with shards of pain. They danced around the cloud, revealing faces filled with pain, regret, sadness, and longing. The horde of spirits had returned to the darkness, absorbed into the black cloud. Their return had allowed the blackness to grow even larger. It filled up the cavern.

Go now.

I nodded and with Martin by my side, I left the sphere of light. It was like stepping into a hurricane. Wind whipped my hair around my face, stinging my cheeks. The cavern was filled with shrieking and screams, and the sound of rushing wind. The cloud spun around, a wild storm boiling with evil.

We took another step forward and the darkness sent out tendrils of smoke that coaxed us along. They cleared the way on the floor, wiping back the hands that reached from the cloud for our help. My breathing was shallow and my legs felt like they weren't attached to me. We made our way down to the edge of the cloud. The noise down here was almost deafening. My eyes burned as the wind pelted me.

I looked over at Martin and he nodded once, his mouth set in a hard line.

I pressed my lips together and opened the locket. It lay in my hands, the woman's portrait staring up at me. She smiled. *Marisssa.* I peered down at her face, the whisper dying in the silence.

The silence.

I looked up.

Everything around me was frozen. The cloud was still and the screaming had stopped. Nothing moved for a long moment. Then, I heard a voice from the darkness.

"Charlotte?"

A figure stepped out from the cloud. It was a man. He was dressed in brown pants and a white shirt. His hat was floppy on his head and he was unshaven. He looked up at me with the bluest eyes I'd ever seen. In slow motion, I watched those eyes change. They went from unbelieving to sadness, to fury. He cried out, an animalistic sound that reverberated against the walls of the cavern.

I backpedaled from the seething anger rising up from him as he lunged for me. I tripped and fell, the locket knocked from my grasp. It clattered to the floor and time froze again. What passed in seconds took several minutes for my mind to process. I saw the minutia of every moment.

Martin gazed down at the locket as it lay open on the ground. His eyes filled with tears and his image wavered. He looked up at me and his hair lengthened, his features softening. The worn clothes he wore changed, the pants winding around his legs into a full hoop skirt and the shirt changing into a white one with lace details on the sleeves. His hair drew up and piled in curls at the top of his head and a soft blush tinged his cheeks.

"Martin?" I whispered.

She turned her attention to me. "This is my mother. Which means…" She turned, facing the man. He was moving through the air, filled with a rage that was directed at me, descending upon me with agonizing slowness. I braced myself and prepared for the impact.

Then she was standing in front of me, between the imminent danger and myself. She looked upon the man from the darkness with a calm countenance and held up a dainty hand toward him, palm out.

He froze mid-lunge, his attention shifting from me to her. His face came into focus and he regarded her. Realization spread across his features. "My daughter?"

He reached out to her from the darkness, the smoke whirling around him, through him.

The woman nodded, her gaze never leaving him as she reached out for his outstretched hand. Her other hand appeared behind her back, and with a flick of her wrist, the locket jumped from the floor into her palm. She closed her fingers around the open locket, the chain dangling from her fist.

He hesitated, his eyes filled with tears. "Is it truly you?"

She nodded again. "It is I, Father."

With that, their hands touched, sending out shards of black smoke into the cavern. The shards screeched past my head, whirring through the silence and breaking upon the walls with a shattering sound like a million glasses breaking. The remaining smoke twisted around them both, gathering them in an embrace of darkness. The black cloud grew, blocking them from my view. With an enormous explosion, the cloud rose up, spreading sadness in its wake. It hovered above the cavern for a moment and then jettisoned into the locket. It snapped closed and fell to the ground.

Savannah. It whispered and then all was quiet again.

The space was filled only with the sound of my breathing for a minute. Two. Then, it came alive. Spirits that had been scattered on the floor by the departure of the darkness were beginning to stand, holding their hands to their heads and mumbling. It looked like the aftermath of a bomb. I felt sick.

Thank you, Marissa.

I spun around to see MingkéHá standing behind me. The light had disappeared from around him.

"Are you okay? Did I break you?"

He reached out to touch my cheek. *That was very brave. Not many can face a choice like that and choose so wisely.*

There was a movement behind me and I turned to see Sam striding toward us. He was thin and his cheeks were gaunt.

I took a protective stance in front of MingkéHá. "Stay behind me," I said out of the corner of my mouth.

He chuckled then looked around me. *Samuel. It is good to see you well again, my friend.*

Sam approached. He took my shoulders in his hands and looked down at me, his eyes searching mine. I withered from his touch as he tried to speak. No sound came out, though. He looked pleadingly at MingkéHá.

Are you certain, my friend? Once the power is given, it cannot be returned.

Sam nodded, his eyes filling with tears. *MingkéHá, you have been the guardian of our town now for many, many years. You must be tired.*

MingkéHá closed his eyes for a moment. When he did, the weight of his choice pressed down on me. I felt tears burn my eyes.

Sam reached out and placed his hand on the man's shoulder. *It is my choice. It is my turn. Let me take this burden from you.*

MingkéHá took a deep breath. *Take care of our people, Samuel.* With that, he reached out to take Sam's hands, warmth spreading through Sam with the touch. The light around them intensified and I held my arm up to shield my eyes. A ball of fire drew up from MingkéHá's chest and hovered above them, pulling strings of energy from his body. The strings circled the ball, twisting in a rainbow of colors that lit up the entire cavern. Sam stared into the man's eyes as the ball released the strings, shooting them down into Sam's body. The ball of light melted, illuminating Sam from the inside out.

He stood up straight, his features returning to normal. Sam turned to me and strode over, grabbing me by the shoulders. "Are you all right? How's your dad? Evie?" He looked the same as when we'd first met, before he went into the darkness. Except for his eyes. They were haunted and more deep set than they'd been before. He also spoke with a lisp, and the corner of his mouth pulled downward, as if he'd had a stroke.

I could feel the emotion pouring off him in waves. I crumpled. "I think they're okay. I sent them out through a portal Grandma and Martin made. But they're all gone now." I felt sobs bubbling up from my core. "Everyone. Andy, he, he went into the darkness to save me. He's gone, too!"

You know it'd take a lot more than that to take me out, Anderson!

I whirled around and saw Andy walking toward me. He was flanked by my grandma, Henry, George, and Alice. Alice's arm was stretched out and she was leading Sarah toward me. Grandma had Grandpa with her. My mind was spinning and I couldn't breathe as I stared down at them.

"You should go to them," Sam said. He brushed my hair from my face. "You did a good thing tonight, Marissa."

I broke from Sam's grasp and ran down the slope toward them, stopping short in front of Andy. I reached up and smacked him in the chest, then grabbed him and pulled him into a hug. I sobbed into his jacket.

You do realize you're the only person on the planet who can get away with that, right?

Oh, shut up and hug me! And don't you ever do anything so stupid again!

I let go of Andy and threw my arms around Grandma. She welcomed me into a hug that felt odd.

Her face was drawn tight and her eyes were guarded. I held her at arm's length.

Grandpa's voice cracked as he murmured over and over again, "Come quick. Marissa's in trouble…" Sarah stared out from vacant eyes, the hair along her temples shot through with a gray that hadn't been there before.

"What's wrong with them?" I turned to Sam, panic tinging the edge of my voice.

Sam came down to stand near me. "It's hardest on spirits, being in there." He jutted his chin toward the space the darkness had occupied. "For some, it will be a long road to come back from, and for some, well," he dropped his gaze, "they might not ever make it all the way out."

"What about you? You were in there for a long time."

"MingkéHá helped to heal me."

"Then have him help everyone else."

"He is done. What he gave me was the last of his power."

I turned to see MingkéHá on his knees, his hair falling limply over his shoulders. He took a deep breath and smiled at me. He got up and turned as the woman I saw in the grove stepped out of the shadows. She smiled and reached out to MingkéHá. He held her in an embrace, and then turned to raise his hand in our direction.

It is my time to go. I am no longer needed here. Take care of your people. All of them. É^e Náwu Pí arámañisge hdaho, hagún da ke. With that, he was gone, disappearing through the wall of the cavern with his wife.

The space seemed lighter somehow and I turned, expecting to see spirits start shooting up out of the cavern to be with their loved ones. Nothing was moving though, only spirits wandering around without purpose. Maybe they were in shock. Maybe I was. I sat down, my legs finally giving out. Andy joined me and Sam picked up the locket from the ground and came to sit beside me. He was practically glowing. I looked closer and realized he really *was* glowing.

"So, you're the new dude in the light, huh?" Andy asked.

Sam squinted and looked at all of the spirits milling around. "I'll continue to do what I do best. Help move them to places where they don't have to be alone anymore." He sighed. "It would have been nice if it had worked, though."

I shook my head. "I don't understand."

"If you had broken the Curse of Culvers Grove."

I shook my head again. "But, we did. We trapped the darkness in the locket. Well, Martin did. Girl version of Martin. Is her name Savannah? I heard the locket whisper Savannah and sometimes it whispers my name so maybe that was her name. But why was she pretending to be a boy?"

For the love of Pete, Anderson, stop talking.

I clamped my lips closed.

"If we'd broken the curse, the spirits would be able to leave. They're all still trapped here, aren't they?" Andy asked.

You can't see them anymore?

Andy shook his head.

"Yep, they are. They are all still here." Sam looked around, shaking his head slowly.

He stood up and handed me the locket. "I have work to do. You go check on your dad. Take them with you." He gestured defeatedly at my family as he walked away.

I looked at Andy, my heart hurting. *I let everyone down.*

He smiled at me. *No, you didn't. Come on; let's go see your dad.*

I looked down at the locket in my hand. Sighing, I placed the chain around my neck again. It felt heavy, sinking into my chest with a weight it didn't have before.

CHAPTER 33

It took the whole night, but we finally got my family back to Sarah's house. I felt guilty about leaving them there, with the walking wounded helping the worst off of the bunch. Grandma assured me they would be fine as she shuffled Grandpa off to bed. Her eyes held no spark, though, and when she hugged me goodbye, the energy was missing.

Andy and I made our way across the field as the rising sun cast a pink glow to the snow. The tracks of Evie, Tristan, Grant, and my dad were visible.

Four sets of prints. That's promising, right?

Andy didn't answer. By the time we could see the gas station on the other side of the trees, the sun was higher in the sky and brought with it a warmth we hadn't felt in a long time. I was glad we had left our heavy winter coats behind in the cave. The crisp air kept me awake. I needed about a gallon of coffee to do the trick, though. I hesitated at the tree line as Andy went to get the truck that someone had dropped off. Probably Tristan. The engine roared to life and he pulled up, leaning over to open the passenger door.

The memory of Grant's hand blistering played in front of my vision as I stood there, my hand clasped around the locket.

If it burns, step back into the barrier. Andy smiled at me. *Duh.*

I nodded and swallowed. I took a tentative step forward and then another. As I passed through the barrier, nothing happened. I climbed into the truck.

"What's it doing?" Andy nodded at my neck.

I looked down to see the locket pulling away from me. It vibrated toward the rising sun. I shook my head and grabbed it, placing it under my shirt as I buckled the seatbelt.

"All good?" Andy asked.

"Yeah, all good."

My heart hurt with the expectancy of seeing my dad, hoping against hope that the time he'd spent down there hadn't affected him like the spirits I saw wandering around in the basement of the courthouse. Lost spirits. Broken spirits.

I shook my head and let it lean against the cold window.

A moment later, Andy was shaking me awake. "We're here."

I looked up. We were parked by the back porch of our house. I shook my head. "What are we doing here?"

He shrugged. "Tristan texted and said they were here."

"But we have to get out of town. It'll make us all sick again."

"I feel fine. Starving, but I'm fine."

I noted the twinge of sadness I felt roll off him, but my attention was pulled to the slamming screen door.

Grant stood on the back porch. He was wearing a blue denim shirt and his hair gleamed in the early morning sun. He tossed his hair out of his eyes and ran down the steps. I shoved open the door and met him halfway, welcoming his arms around me. He leaned down to kiss me and I melted against him.

Andy left us outside while he ran into the house. "Tristan!"

"Are you okay?" Grant held me at arm's length and looked me up and down.

"I just want to see my dad."

A line creased Grant's brow.

"What?"

"You have to be prepared for what you're going to see. He's been through a lot and it's going to take…"

I didn't hear the rest of his sentence because I broke away from him and bounded up the steps and through the back door.

"Dad!" I skidded to a stop at the living room doorway.

Evie sat next to my dad on the couch, a blanket over their legs. She was sleeping, with her head slumped onto his shoulder as the fire crackled in the wood stove. His eyes were open and staring straight ahead. I crossed the floor and perched on the couch. I reached out and took his hand. It was cold.

"Dad?"

He turned to look at me. "Hey, Peanut." Then he turned back and stared ahead.

I spun my mom's ring on my finger and loosened it. Pulling it off my own finger, I placed my mom's ring in his palm and closed his fingers around it. He glanced down and then up at me again.

"Hey, Peanut."

I started to cry. Grant helped me upstairs and into the shower. I left the locket on. My tears mingled with the water droplets as I washed. The locket was heavy on my chest. When I turned the water off, his hand jutted through the space between the shower curtain and the wall, handing me a white fluffy towel. I wrapped myself in it and he gave me a pair of warm pajamas from the drawer. By the time I crawled into my bed next to him, I had almost cried myself out. Now, I was on to hiccupping.

Grant held me, smoothing back my hair all day. He would rub my cheek softly when I woke up with a nightmare.

By the evening, I woke up and stretched. It was snowing and Grant smiled as he woke up, too.

"Morning, sunshine," he said.

"Morning," I mumbled. The locket was a constant pressure on my chest now.

"St. Louis!" Evie burst through my door. "Oh! Sorry!" She averted her eyes.

"We're both dressed." I rolled my eyes. "What's up?"

"You have to come see this!" She disappeared.

"What's going on?"

"I don't know, but let me hold you for six more seconds before I have to let you go." He peppered me with a kiss for each second he counted then hugged me to him. "It's all going to be okay. We'll get through this."

When we got downstairs, Evie was standing in the space between the kitchen and the dining room. I came up next to her and wrinkled my nose.

"What *is* that?"

"Smells like something died, came back to life, ate a bushel of onions, and then died again," Andy said from the living room where he and Tristan were curled on the couch together.

I turned to find the source of the smell. My dad stood at the stove, pushing something around a frying pan with a fork. I walked over.

"Hey, Peanut. How are you?"

I glanced up at him. "Um, fine. How are you?"

He didn't answer and kept moving the mush around in the pan. It looked like oatmeal and ham mixed with soy sauce.

"What did I have to see?" I asked Evie.

"He's cooking!"

I looked back at my dad. "He never cooks."

"Amend that - he *likes* to cook. He sucks at it, though." She sat down at the table and chewed on the end of a straw.

I took pity on him and directed him away from the stove and to the table. I poured him a bowl of cereal and handed him a spoon. "Eat," I directed.

He followed directions, and lifted the spoon to his mouth, milk dribbling down his chin. After eating, I got him upstairs while Evie cleaned up the mess in the kitchen. I tucked my dad into his bed and sat down on the edge.

How many times am I going to be in this same place? I tried to help them all and I keep failing. Over and over again.

I felt something touch my hand and I looked down to see my dad's hand on mine. I looked over at him, tears springing to my eyes.

"Hey, Peanut," he said. He smiled at me and patted my hand. "I'll see you in the morning."

He lay back and closed his eyes. I watched him for a long time as his breathing grew deep and even. Finally, I got up and pulled the blanket up to his chest.

"Night, Dad," I said, leaning down to kiss his cheek. "Love you."

"Love you, too, Peanut," he mumbled before rolling over and starting to snore.

I left the hallway light on and his door cracked before heading downstairs. Everyone was in the living room.

Evie looked up. "Is he asleep?"

I nodded, pressing my lips together. I stepped over Andy's legs to sit down on the couch. I settled into the cushion. Grant put his arm around me and squeezed.

Evie cleared her throat. "Are you going to tell us what happened down there after you guys sabotaged us?"

Andy and I took turns filling them in on the events of the previous night. Tristan listened quietly, his eyes never leaving Andy's face. I could feel something rising up from him and I looked over at Evie. Her lips were drawn into a thin line as she stared at Tristan.

Andy tossed a handful of popcorn in his mouth. "Anderson thinks that Martin's real name was Savannah."

"I've heard it say my name. I thought maybe it was the woman's name." I rubbed my eyes. "I don't know what to think. I wish I could talk to him."

"Why don't you?" Tristan asked.

The room grew silent.

"How?" Andy stared at him.

Tristan shrugged. "Hold the locket and ask him."

"I can only see the past, though." Andy shook his head.

"How do you know?"

Andy regarded him for a moment and then let out a laugh like a bark. He sat up. "All right, Anderson, let's give this one a try."

I nodded. Grasping the locket firmly, I pulled it out from under my shirt. It immediately pulled away from my chest, pointing toward the back of the house. "I don't know what's up with it," I sighed.

Andy's hand closed around the locket. He blinked several times and then looked wide-eyed up at me.

"I do," he said, breathlessly. "It-it wants to go home. To Savannah."

I shook my head. "Savannah?"

Georgia.

Andy stood up and looked around, a smile spreading on his face. "So, who's up for a road trip?"

Acknowledgements

Thank you to my husband and daughter. Your support and love mean the world to me.

My heartfelt appreciation goes to my friend, Christina Benedict, for helping to mold this story into shape, to my amazing beta readers, Roger Bolle and Julie Bolle, for their support and input, to my wonderful editor, Frankie Sutton, for her feedback and attention to detail, to Covered Creatively for another beautiful cover design, and to Vicki Deiter for her formatting expertise.

I also want to express my sincerest appreciation to Jimm G. Goodtracks, author and editor of the Ioway-Otoe-Missouria (Baxoje-Jiwere-Ñut^achi) Language Project and Dictionary, whose kind assistance, expertise, and input were essential to the research and writing of this book.

About The Author

Adria Waters is the author of the Ghost Hunters Society series and has seen ghosts all her life. She loves exploring the paranormal and goes on ghost tours in every place she visits. When she's not hunting ghosts, she loves torturing her family with road trips across the country to see every single sightseeing opportunity in the United States. Adria lives in Missouri with her very patient husband, her not-so-patient daughter, a herd of cats who insist that they are human, and various little spirits that pop up to say "hello" once in a while.

You can find out more about Adria and her
writing at
www.AdriaWaters.com

www.ingramcontent.com/pod-product-compliance
Lightning Source LLC
Chambersburg PA
CBHW070625260626
47161CB00007B/2589